LIE
LE.

D1429439

THE BOY
IS BACK IN TOWN

THE BOY
IS BACK IN TOWN

BY

NINA HARRINGTON

First published in Great Britain 2011
by Mills & Boon, an imprint of Harlequin (UK) Limited.
Large Print edition 2012
Harlequin (UK) Limited, Eton House,
18-24 Paradise Road, Richmond, Surrey TW9 1SR

© Nina Harrington 2011

ISBN: 978 0 263 22564 8

Harlequin (UK) policy is to use papers that are natural, renewable and recyclable products and made from wood grown in sustainable forests. The logging and manufacturing process conform to the legal environmental regulations of the country of origin.

Printed and bound in Great Britain
by CPI Antony Rowe, Chippenham, Wiltshire

CHAPTER ONE

MARIGOLD CHANCE scrolled through the images on her digital camera with her thumb, and cringed. Of all the crimes against photography she had ever committed for her sister Rosa, of which there had been many, the past few hours had been a low point.

Mari might be forgiven for the portrait of the dry cleaner's miniature dachshund in a cute beaded princess sweater, or even the popcorn-puff hooded jacket Rosa had made for the hairdresser's Pekinese. But persuading the news-agent's fox terrier to pose with a knitted plaid waterproof raincoat with the name 'Lola' in gold chain stitch on the back was the last straw.

Her sister Rosa had a lot to answer for.

'Oh, you are such a genius.' Rosa grabbed the sleeve of Mari's coat and squealed so loudly that two elderly ladies in the street looked across in alarm. Mari gave them a smile and a small wave with the hand that was not firmly in the fierce grip of her sister, the budding internet entrepreneur, who was wrestling to see the back of the camera.

'Lola looks amazing. You see? I knew it would be useful to have an IT expert in the family one day. You told me how important it was to have great visuals on the website you made for me and now I have. It was hard work but so worth it.'

Mari snorted in reply and lifted the camera out of her sister's reach. 'You spent most of the time lying on the floor playing with the puppy and feeding her treats. I was the one doing the hard work.'

Rosa waggled her fingers at her dismissively. 'What can I say? Some of us are blessed with the creative touch. Animal models are hard to find in the world of Swanhaven pet fashion and Lola wasn't too keen on posing for more than a few seconds. I think bribery is acceptable in the circumstances. After all, it's not often my big sister has a chance to be a fashion photographer for the day. The least I could do was sacrifice my dignity in the name of your future career. You might need that extra line on your résumé one day soon.'

Mari sighed and gave her head a quick shake. 'I should never have told you that my department is laying off technical staff. I'm fine. *Seriously.* There are lots of hardware engineers who want to take the package and do other things with their lives, but not me. I love what I'm doing and don't plan to change any time soon.'

'Um…fine. Right. Is that why you were looking for IT jobs around Swanhaven on the internet this morning?'

'Hey!' Mari play poked Rosa in the arm. 'Were you spying on me, young lady? I can see behind that sweet innocent face, you know.' Mari paused for a moment and decided to give Rosa a half version of the truth. 'I wanted to compare the freelance rates in Dorset compared to California, that's all,' she replied with a smile and shrug. 'Things have certainly changed a lot in the years since I last lived here. Apparently there's Wi-Fi in the yacht club. Could this really be possible?'

And the moment the words had left her mouth, Mari instantly felt guilty about not telling her only sister the full truth. But she couldn't reveal her secret just yet, no matter how much she was looking forward to seeing the look on Rosa's face when she broke the news that she was buying back their childhood home. Rosa had been inconsolable when their little family of women had been evicted from the home where they'd once been so happy, and Mari knew how much she'd wanted to live there again.

But she couldn't even hint that the house could be theirs until she was certain that everything was in place.

Rosa was sensitive enough to pick up that Mari was worried about her job security and with good reason. Mari Chance had been the provider in this family since the age of sixteen, when their father had left and their mother floundered in grief and despair.

It had been Mari's decision to sacrifice her

dreams of university so that she could leave school as soon as she could to work for a local business and become the breadwinner for Rosa and their mother. And she felt even more responsible now that Rosa was on her own and she had a high-flying job with a salary to make sure that Rosa was taken care of. Even if it did mean that they were apart—her sister had to come first before anything that Mari wanted in her own life.

Rosa was the only person in Mari's life who she truly trusted but this was one time when she wasn't ready to open up and share her fears and dreams for the future. She had worked too hard to give Rosa hope, only to see it replaced with bitter disappointment.

Luckily her sister was distracted by a lovely spaniel who dared to be out in the cold air without one of her knitted coats and, spotting a potential customer, Rosa pulled Mari closer and whispered, 'See you back at the cottage. I'm on a mission. Bye for now. Oh—and thanks again for the photographs. I knew I could rely on you.

We'll talk more later.' And with that, she released Mari all in a rush and scampered off in the direction of the spaniel, her hand already in her pocket looking for dog treats.

'You're welcome, sweetie,' Mari replied in a low whisper nobody was going to hear as she watched Rosa laugh and smile with the spaniel's lady owner. 'You know you can always rely on me.'

Marigold Chance was never the girl called for sports teams or talent contests. She'd left that to her brilliant older brother Kit and her little sister Rosa. Both extroverts to the core. No, Mari was the person who'd stayed in the background and made the teas and watched the other people having fun. Usually at events she had organised and made happen. Every family needed a Mari to keep things working behind the scenes to make sure that everyone was safe and well and had what they needed. No matter how great the personal cost.

Especially in times of crisis when the whole world fell apart.

Mari shrugged off a shiver of sad memories, turned the corner and started down the narrow cobbled street towards the harbour, and was rewarded by the sight she never grew tired of—Swanhaven bay stretched out in front of her.

The sea was a wide expanse of dove-grey, flecked by bright white foam as the waves picked up in the icy wind. A bright smile warmed Mari's face despite the cold. Swanhaven harbour had been built of granite blocks designed to protect the fishing fleet from the harsh English Channel. Now the long wide arms held more pleasure craft than local fishermen, but it was still a safe harbour and delightful marina which attracted visitors all year round, even on a cold February afternoon.

But that was not where she wanted to go before the early winter darkness fell. There was somewhere very special she wanted to visit now she was free for the rest of the day. The one place that meant more to her and Rosa than anywhere else in the world. She could hardly wait to see her old home again. Snow or no snow. Nothing was going to stop her now. Nothing at all.

'Well, you know what your father's like. Once he gets an idea in his head, nothing is going to stop him.' His mother chuckled down Ethan Chandler's cellphone, her voice faint and in snatches as it was carried away in the blustery wind. 'He's out by the pool at the moment and quite determined to experiment with all of the fancy extras on his new barbecue, even if we are in the middle of a mini heatwave. Which reminds me. How *is* the weather in Swanhaven at the moment?'

Ethan Chandler took a firm grip with his other hand on the tiller of the small sailing boat he had hired from the Swanhaven sailing school and let the fresh wind carry the light boat out from his private jetty into deeper water before answering. A spray of icy sea water crashed over the side of the boat and he moved the phone closer towards his mouth and under the shelter of his jacket.

'You'll be delighted to know that at the moment it is grey, wet and windy. And cold. Cold by

Florida standards at least. You're going to freeze next week.'

Her reply was a small sigh. 'I did wonder. I remember only too well what February can be like. But don't you worry. Your father and I wouldn't miss seeing our new holiday home for anything. We are so proud of you, Ethan.'

Ethan inhaled a slow calming breath. *Proud?* Proud was the last thing his parents should be.

Far from it.

Apart from a couple of one-to-one sailing classes he had run as a personal favour to his old mentor at the Swanhaven Yacht Club, he had made it his business to keep out of sight and hide away at the house. The work that needed to be done was an excellent excuse for not socialising in the town but, the truth was, in a small town like Swanhaven, people had long memories. Ten years was nothing, and Kit Chance still had a lot of family in the area and the weight of the accident which killed Kit had become heavier and heavier the longer he stayed here.

Proud? No. The minute his parents were settled, he would be on the first flight back to Florida.

Luckily his mother did not give him a chance to reply. 'And how are you managing at the house on your own?'

Ethan turned his head back towards the shore and enjoyed a half smile at the sight of the stunning one-storey home which hugged the wooded hillside on one side and the wide curve of the inlet on the other. Now that was something he *could* be proud of.

It was a superb location. Quiet, private and secluded but only ten minutes drive to Swanhaven, which lay around the headland in the next bay, and even faster by boat. Perfect.

'Everything's fine. I'm just heading out now to Swanhaven to pick up some groceries. But don't worry, Mum. The team have done a great job and it will all be ready for next weekend.' *I hope.*

'That's wonderful, darling. You've been so secretive these past few months; I can hardly wait to see what you've done with the place. And don't you worry about your father. I know he was reluctant at first to let you manage the project, but you know how hard it is for him to hand over control of anything to anybody. He's so pleased that you agreed to finish off the work for us. We both are. Who knows? With a bit of luck your father might actually start slowing down and think about retirement one day soon.'

Ethan fought down a positive reply but the words stuck in his throat.

It had taken a few years before his parents understood that their only son had no interest in becoming the fourth generation architect in Chandler and Chandler, Architects. Ethan had no intention of spending his life in an air-conditioned office looking out on the ocean when he could be on the waves himself, pushing himself harder and harder. He felt sorry to let them down but they eventually accepted the fact that he had his own life to lead and they had supported him as best they could.

The least he could do was come over to Swanhaven and finish off their retirement home for them. It was ironic that his mother had chosen to come back to Swanhaven of all places, but she had grown up in the area and they had some happy memories of the summers they spent here before the accident which changed all of their lives. His most of all.

They had talked about Swanhaven many times and he knew that, although his mother loved this bay, they had chosen not to come back here because of the accident and how he felt about it.

But now they were ready to move on and this house was a symbol of that.

And if they could cope with having a holiday home here, then he would have to learn to live with that. It was the moving part that he had a problem with. But that was his problem, not theirs, and there was no way he was going to spoil his mother's delight in her new house.

'Good luck with that one, Mum. If anyone can do it, you can.'

'Well, thank you for that vote of confidence. Oh, I'm now being called to ogle some gizmo or gadget. Keep safe, darling. And see you next Saturday. Keep safe.'

Keep safe. That was what she used to say at the dockside before he set out on a dangerous sea journey. They were always her final words. Only a year ago they had been squeezed out through tears when he left for the Green Globe round-the-world race. Now he could hear warmth and an almost casual tone in her voice through the broken reception.

So much had changed. Now she was saying it before a short shopping trip across the bay to Swanhaven, not months spent alone battling the most treacherous oceans in the world where a simple mistake could cost him the boat or his life. Or both. Where he could be out of contact with the world for hours. Perhaps days.

Now she could call him from the kitchen of their lovely Florida home and know precisely where he would be for at least six months of the year. Safe and out of harm's way. Running sailing courses at the international yacht club where troubled teenagers from all over the state could receive the help they needed to rebuild their lives.

And she was happier than he had seen her for a long time.

How could she understand that he had chosen to abandon his comfortable car in Swanhaven and come out in wild wet weather in a boat which was smaller than the one he used to have as a boy, just to feel the wind and the spray? To sense the reaction of the rudder under his hand as the tiny sail stretched out to the fullest it had probably ever seen as he angled the craft into the wind at just the perfect inclination to squeeze every drop of speed.

He knew this stretch of water like the back of his own hand. Kit had shown him where the currents lay over shallow water and the best place to turn into the wind so that they could practice how to use the sails.

Ethan smiled to himself and shifted the tiller just a little more. Just seeing this part of the bay again on his first day had brought back so many fine memories, and some sad ones. Those summers spent sailing every day with Kit Chance had been some of the happiest times of his life. And he still missed him.

Over the past year or two his mother had dropped not so subtle questions about when he planned to stop pushing himself harder and harder with each yacht race. He had always laughed it off. But she had a point. Maybe there was more to life than competitive sailing? But he had not found it yet. Teaching kids to sail for a few months a year had done nothing to lessen his need to be at the helm of a boat, on his own, testing the boundaries, running faster and faster. But it was a start.

Kit would have loved it. But he couldn't. Because he had died in a freak accident nobody could have predicted or prevented. And Ethan had survived. The burden of that guilt still lay heavy on his shoulders. Especially in this town where Kit had grown up. So far he had managed to keep a low profile and focus on the work at hand.

Ethan shrugged the tension away from his shoulders.

He had seven days to finish the house before his parents flew into London, then he would get back to honouring Kit in the only way he knew how. By sailing to the max and teaching young people how to live their lives to the full, just as Kit had done.

With a bit of luck his parents might actually like what he had done. Especially when they found out that he had made a couple of alterations to the original plans. Instead of an extended parking area, Ethan had built a solid garage, workshop, boathouse and jetty. These were his personal gifts to his parents. And particularly his father.

Maybe, just maybe, they could find the time to sail out on their own boat together from their private jetty, like they used to, when he came back in July to make good his promise to open the Swanhaven regatta.

Now that was something worth looking forward to.

A squall of icy sleet hit Ethan straight in the face and he roared with laughter and dropped his head back in joy. That was more like it. Bring it on. Bring. It. On.

* * *

Marigold Chance thrust her hands deep inside the pockets of her thick padded down coat and braced herself against the freezing wind, which was whipping up the sand onto the path that led away from Swanhaven and out past the marina and jetty to the wild part of the Dorset shoreline.

Leaving the village behind, she walked as fast as she could to get warm, her target already in sight. A slow winding path started on the shore then rose slowly up and onto the grassy banks onto the low chalk hills which became cliffs at the other end of the bay.

Steps had been cut into the cliff face from the beach, but Mari paused and closed her eyes for a moment before she stepped forward, desperate to clear her head and try to relieve the throbbing headache which had been nagging at the back of her neck for the past twenty-four hours.

This part of the beach was made up of pebbles which had been smoothed by the relentless action of the waves back and forth to form fine powder sand in places and large cobblestones in others. It had been snowing when she arrived in

Swanhaven and the air was still cold enough to keep the snow in white clumps on top of the frozen ice trapped between the stones at the top end of the beach where she was walking. The heavy winter seas carried with them pieces of drift-wood and seaweed that floated in the cold waters of a shipping lane like the English Channel.

For once Mari was glad to feel the cold fresh wind buffeting her cheeks as she snuggled low inside the warm coat, a windproof hat pulled well down over her ears.

The relentless pressure of her job as a computer systems trouble-shooter was starting to get to her, but exhaustion came with the job and it was all worth it. In a few years she would be able to start her own business and work from home as an internet consultant. With modern technology, she could work from home and run an online internet advisory business from anywhere in the world, and that included Swanhaven. This small coastal town where she had spent the first eigh-teen years of her life was where she wanted to make a life and create a stable, long-standing home, safe and warm, for herself and Rosa. A home nobody could take away from her. From either of them.

Mari inhaled slowly to calm her breathing and focused on the sound of the seagulls calling above her head, dogs barking on the shore and the relentless beat of the waves.

She could still hear the flap of the pennants on the boats in the marina and the musical sound of the wind in the rigging of the sailing boats.

This was the soundtrack of her early life, which had stayed with her no matter where she might be living and working. Here she could escape the relentless cacophony of cars, aircraft engines, noisy air conditioning and frantic telephone calls in the middle of the night from IT departments whose servers had crashed. In her shoulder bag there were three smartphones and two mobile phones. But right now, for one whole precious hour, she had turned everything off.

And it was bliss. Her breathing tuned into the rhythm of the ebb and flow of the waves on the shore and for a fraction of a second she felt as though she was a girl again and she had never left Swanhaven.

Sailing and the sea had formed a fundamental part of her childhood. She loved the sea with a passion. She knew how cruel it could be, but there was no finer place in the world. And Kit would understand that.

Turning her back to the wind, Mari slipped the glove from her left hand and reached into the laptop bag she carried everywhere. Her fingers touched a precious photograph and she carefully drew it out of the bag, holding tightly so that it would not be snatched away in the gusty wind. It was only right that she should look at this photograph here of all places, even though it had been around the world with her more than once. Not like Kit's best friend Ethan Chandler, on the deck of some horrendously expensive racing yacht, battling the ocean for his very life, but inside a bag which went into the cabins of aircraft and hotel rooms and even restaurants and offices and computer server rooms.

The smiling face of her mother looked back at

her from the photograph. She was a tall, slim, pretty woman with freckled skin illuminated by the sunlight reflected back from the water in the sunny harbour of Swanhaven. One of her arms was draped around Rosa's shoulders. Rosa must have been about fourteen then and so full of life and fun and energy. Her baby sister was always ready to smile into the camera without a hint of embarrassment or hesitation. But this time Rosa and her mother had something to laugh about—because they were watching Kit playing the fool. As always. Seventeen years old and full of mischief, Kit was their hero, full of life and energy and funny, handsome and charming—everyone loved him, and he was indulged and spoiled. Kit would not sit still for a moment, always jumping about, always wanting to be in the action, especially when it came to the water and sailing.

Mari remembered the day she'd taken the photograph so well. It was the Easter holiday and the sailing club had been open for a training day. Of course Kit was the instructor, yet again, but he was not content to simply smile for his younger sister, but had to leap forward onto one knee and wave jazz hands at her, which, of course, made Rosa and her mother laugh even louder. This was her happy family she loved, so natural and so unrehearsed. Just a typical shot of a mum having fun with her three kids on a trip to the marina.

Looking at the image now, she could almost feel the sun on her face and the wind in her hair on that April morning when she'd captured the precious moment in time when they'd all been so happy together. It was hard to believe that she had taken the photograph only a few months before the yacht race in the annual Swanhaven Sailing Regatta when they lost Kit in a freak accident and the thin fabric of safe, loving little family was ripped apart.

He had been the golden boy. The much-loved only son.

Oh, Kit. She missed him so much, like a physical ache that never truly went away, but somehow over the years she had learned to push it to the back of her mind so that she could survive every day, though the pain of the loss was still there.

Coming back to Swanhaven, and seeing the boats in the marina and young people finding such joy in the water, brought back all of those happy memories so vividly.

They had been such good times with her family all around her.

Mari ran her fingertip down her mother's face on the photograph, just as the wind picked up and almost whipped it away, and she popped it back into her bag, made sure that it was safe and pulled on her gloves as quickly as she could.

Perhaps she was not as ready to see her old home as she thought she was? It had been her mother's dream that one day she should be able to buy back the home she had loved so very much, but she'd died before Mari could help to make that dream come true. And it broke Mari's heart to think that she had let her down when they had come so close to making it a reality.

But she still had Rosa to take care of, so she drove herself to work harder and longer to help her sister, no matter what the cost to her own dreams of running her own business.

Turning away from the cliff, Mari faced the wild buffeting wind from the sea and skipped down the path back onto the shore, walking faster and faster along the rough large boulders, sliding on the wet surface, squelching against kelp seaweed, until she was at the end of the jetty and in front of her was the curving bay and the rising cliffs of chalk towering above in the distance.

She took a couple of steps further along the beach and there it was, the low dip in the cliff made by a small river and the sloping grassy bank and the winding path from the shore which led to the cottages where they used to live. Bracing herself, Mari lifted her head, back to the wind, and looked up towards the houses she could see quite clearly now. At this distance, the aged and weathered old roofs blocked the view of the actual house itself, but she could see a large placard from the local estate agent announcing that the house was soon to be sold by auction and the contact details. She had talked to the elderly couple who owned it a few times, but they had not been interested in selling. Until now, when a broken hip had forced them to move into the village.

Tears pricked her eyes and she wiped them away with the finger of her glove. Cold wind and regret assaulted her eyes. But her mouth sheltered a secret smile.

It had taken years of working nights, week-ends and public holidays for the extra salary she needed to build up savings but she had finally done it this week after her bonus for working over the whole Christmas and New Year holiday had been paid. It was hard to believe that she finally had enough for the deposit she needed to buy back the house their father had built brick by brick. This was probably the only chance she would have to make this house a home again for herself and her sister, where they could live and work side by side one day.

Other people had social lives. Lovely homes and designer clothing. Even boyfriends. Instead, Mari Chance had become the 'go to' single girl who was willing to work when her colleagues spent precious holiday time with their families.

Promotion after promotion had meant travelling to some far-flung parts of the world at a moment's notice. But she did it. And most of the time she loved her work. Loved the idea that she could arrive at a business office where the staff were panicking and walk out with the IT system working perfectly. That was deeply satisfying. Besides, she did not have any personal commitments, not even a pet. But all that travel came with a price.

The crushing loneliness.

And now the one thing she had been dreaming about for the last three years was finally going to happen—it was so close, she could almost feel it. Everything was ready. She had the funds, her place at the auction had been booked, and she knew the going rate for the property from recent sales figures.

This was the house she had been born in. The house she had loved and been so happy in, and now she could make the offer—in cash and above the expected price with a loan facility already agreed at the bank, if the price was higher than she had budgeted for.

She had to have this house.

She had to.

This was where her travelling and relentless activity and exhausting work was finally going to come to an end. This was where she was going to spend the rest of her life. Building a routine with Rosa in the place where she had grown up with extended family all around her. She was ready to come home to Swanhaven.

At that moment an icy blast ran up inside Mari's coat and a deep shiver crossed her shoulders and down her back, making her stamp her feet and clap her hands together to restore some circulation. Time to get back to hot tea and toasted crumpets—Rosa's favourites. She could come back and see the house any time she wanted—but perhaps not today.

Indulging in a brief smile and a final lingering look, Mari turned back into the wind as she strolled back towards the marina and the stone terraced cottage Rosa had made her own. In-

stantly Mari's eyes were drawn to a small sailing
boat which was coming towards the jetty from
the west. It was the only boat on the sea and was
too small to have crossed the Channel so it could
not have come very far.

For a moment Mari wondered who was brave
enough, or foolish enough, to be sailing in open
waters on a day like this. Icy blustery wind and
grey skies did not equate in her mind to a pleas-
ant sailing experience. She continued walking,
her head angled down against the wind, but she
could not miss the small craft as it came closer
and closer towards the shore and the safety of a
berth in the sheltered marina. She walked swiftly
to try and get warm but, even with her fast pace
the stiff wind in the small white sail sped the
light craft faster than she could walk.

It was coming in too fast. Much too fast. The
closer she got to the marina, the faster the boat
came towards her. He had not even lowered the
sail and, oh, no, the crosswind was gusting now
across the entrance to the marina. There was
no way this boat could stop itself from being

smashed against the jetty or the stone breakwater of the marina.

No! She had to do something. Shout. Call for help.

Mari looked frantically around—but there was nobody close enough to hear her call and the wind would snatch away any chance of being heard in the town.

The cellphone was useless—the lifeboat would never come out in time. There were only seconds to spare before the boat collided with the dock.

She started jogging, running for the shore, waving her arms above her head, trying frantically to attract the attention of the sailor, who seemed to be totally oblivious to the danger he was in. Mari was shouting now, over and over, 'Watch out, watch out,' but the words were flung back into her face by the bitterly cold winds which attacked her cheeks and eyes so that she could hardly see with the tears of winter blurring her vision. Her hat was long gone, blown away in the wind.

Her heart was beating so fast that she thought

she was going to pass out. Heaving lungfuls of cold air tipped with icy sleet, she reached the edge of the water and had to bend over at the waist, a hand on each knee, not daring to watch as the small boat was tossed violently from side to side like a plastic bath toy.

She knew exactly what was going to happen next and the horror of what was to come filled her mind. She could not watch.

Her face screwed up in pain, ready for the terrible sound of the hull smashing against the jetty, her hands ready to press against her ears to block out the horror and the cries of anguish from the lone sailor. Eyes closed, she knew what was coming and yet felt so powerless to prevent it that the horror of the moment washed over her with a cold shiver which ran across her shoulders and down her back.

She waited and the seconds seemed to stretch into minutes.

And then the minutes grew longer. And all she could hear was the smashing of the waves on the shore and the screeching of the herring gulls as they swooped down into the harbour in the wind.

Slowly, slowly, hardly daring to look, Mari lifted her head and pushed herself to a standing position.

Just in time to see a tall sailor step off his boat onto the jetty, coil the rope around a bollard on the pontoon one-handed and use his other hand to rake his fingers from his forehead back through his hair as if the wind had made a nuisance of itself by messing up his hairstyle.

The sail was down and neatly wrapped, the boat was perfectly aligned in a berth in calm waters and the sailor looked so composed he might have just stepped from a cruise ship on a lazy summer afternoon.

Stunned and totally bewildered, Mari could only watch in amazed silence as the man double-checked the rope, glanced at his watch and then turned around to stroll casually away from her down the walkway which led back to the town.

And just for a second she saw his face for the first time.

Her heart missed a beat.

Ethan Chandler was back in town.

CHAPTER TWO

MARI lifted her head so she could look at Ethan again, just to make sure that she was not mistaken, except this time with her mouth half open in shock.

But of course it was him. Nobody else came even close to Ethan in looks or ability. He had sailed on his own around the world non-stop! Little wonder that he could moor a small boat on a floating pontoon in an English winter.

Ethan… She was looking at Ethan Chandler.

A bolt of energy hit her hard in the stomach and punched the air from her lungs. The blast was so physical that Mari clutched hold of the edge of the stone wall of the marina with both hands to stop herself from sliding onto her knees. Frozen with shock.

She could not believe this was happening. It

had to be some sort of crazy nightmare brought on by lack of sleep and far too much caffeine and wine last night over dinner with Rosa.

There was nothing else to explain it.

The man-boy she had last seen ten years ago looking back at her from the backseat of his father's car as they drove out of Swanhaven, leaving her behind, clinging to the wreckage of her life, was blocking her way back into town. Mari sucked in oxygen to feed her racing brain and the frantic pulsing of blood.

This must be what it felt like to have a heart attack.

The last person on the planet she had expected to see again was dressed in chinos and a pale blue shirt, under a luxurious all-weather jacket the colour of the smoothest latte.

Ethan Chandler. International Yachtsman of the Year. The boy whose family had rented the house next to her home each summer holiday and in the process became part of Swanhaven and the star of the sailing club for a few weeks and her home town's only true claim for a celebrity. The village shop even sold bottles of the delectable designer aftershave he'd promoted a few years earlier.

The stylist who had chosen his shirt had done an excellent job and that particular shade of blue was a perfect match for the colour of his eyes, even in the grey February light which took the edge off a suntan cultivated under the Florida sunshine.

At the age of seventeen Ethan Chandler had been the best-looking boy in town. A natural athlete and champion yachtsman destined for greatness. Ethan at twenty-eight was a revelation. Of course she had seen his photo on TV and on the cover of magazines, clean and polished and with all of his rough edges smoothed out to create the perfect image. Male-model handsome, rugged and broad-shouldered.

But there was a world of difference between seeing Ethan standing behind the wheel of an ocean-going yacht, or modelling board shorts on the cover of a sailing magazine, and having the man himself standing so close that she could see the stubble on his cheek on the side of his face.

Ethan had always had that cocky and easy confidence in his own charm—but this was taking it to a completely new level. Six feet of broadshouldered, tousle-haired hunk could do that to a girl.

The blood rushing to her cheeks and neck was so embarrassing. And Marigold Chance did not blush. Ever.

And then, almost as if he knew that someone was watching him, Ethan stopped walking, paused, and started to turn around to look in her direction.

Instantly, without thinking about what she was doing or hesitating more than a split second, Mari pulled the hood of her coat high over her head and whirled on one heel so quickly that she was walking back the way she had come along the beach path before her hands were back by her sides, punching the air with each step.

Determined to get as far away from Ethan Chandler as possible.

Grains of sand flew up beneath her feet as she

strode forward, too terrified to look back just
in case Ethan had recognised the crazy woman
power walking along the beach. Her head was
spinning with a confusion of thoughts and feelings. Some deep part of her was secretly hoping
that he had seen her, and he was even now running to catch up with her, ready to calm her
nerves and tell her that he'd never meant to hurt
her feelings all those years ago when they had
kissed and he had walked away without a single
word of goodbye.

But that would mean that he had cared about
her back then. And still did. This was impossible.

No. Ethan was always destined to be her brother's unobtainable best friend and the boy who'd
survived the accident when Kit had not.

Her feet slowed but her heart was pounding
inside her chest and she felt the blood flare in
her face despite the icy-cold wind from the sea.
A few more steps and she would be around
the corner of the bay and out of sight from

Swanhaven marina. And Ethan would not be able to see her tears.

Mari's left hand pressed against the damp cliff wall.

After all these years, she had fooled herself into thinking that she had finally come to terms with Kit's death.

Idiot.

All it took was one sight of Ethan—not even a word—just seeing him again, and she was right back to being sixteen again and those terrible few months after the accident when all she wanted to do was be alone. Grieving, scared, frozen and numb and so very alone. Trapped inside her thoughts, withdrawn and traumatised.

Only one person had been able to challenge her enough to break through the prison doors of her anguish and that person was Ethan. He had done something no one had ever done. He had kept challenging, kept on asking her forgiveness, kept on forcing her to engage with him, until her self-imposed barriers had finally broken down. And for one hour of one day she had clung to

Ethan like a drowning girl with every single emotion raw and open and exposed for him to see. This was the boy who had made her brother go out in a race he was not ready for. This was the boy who had teased her and ridiculed her every summer holiday. This was the boy she had secretly had a crush on, but said nothing. Because he was so perfect, so admirable and so very, very unobtainable.

And in that moment when she had been most vulnerable, he had kissed her. And she had kissed him back. And she might have been sixteen, and this was her first kiss, but she knew that he meant it.

And it had destroyed her.

The guilt of kissing and wanting Ethan after he had brought about her family's ruin had been too much for her to bear. She had felt so weak and angry and disgusted with herself.

When he'd left town the following day, without even saying goodbye, she knew that she had deluded herself into thinking that Ethan could ever care about her. She wasn't even worth taking the time to speak to.

Mari closed her eyes and took a couple of long breaths. She was twenty-six years old, a trained IT professional and an adult who was used to handling computer crises. Ethan was probably only passing through with his parents. She could cope with seeing him again over the next few days before she went back to work. It was all going to be fine. Just fine.

Only at the exact same moment she allowed herself to breathe normally, there was the sound of footsteps on the cobblestones and sand and, as she turned her head sideways, Ethan Chandler jogged around the corner.

He tried to slide to a halt on the uneven path, arms flailing at the same time as Mari pushed herself back against the wall.

So the only thing he had to grab hold of to stop himself from falling…was her.

Seconds later, Mari's brain connected to the fact that Ethan Chandler was holding her by both arms, pressing her against his jacket, and she looked up into the blue eyes of the boy who had broken her heart. Words were impossible. Mari inhaled a heady mix of aromatic spices, leather and freshly laundered linen as her own hand moved instinctively to press against the soft fabric and feel the warmth of the man beneath.

'Hello, Mari. Are you okay there? I wondered if it was you.' Ethan flicked his head back towards the shore. 'I only caught a glimpse so I couldn't be sure but…wow…I had no idea you were back in town. I…er…' he broke off as their eyes locked; it was only for a second but she knew that he had recognised the total confusion and disbelief and anger that was whirling around inside her head at seeing him again '…wasn't expecting to see you.'

His iron grip relaxed on the sleeve of her jacket and she almost fell back onto the rocks.

'Ethan,' she whispered, her voice hoarse and pathetic, 'I didn't know that you were around.'

She swallowed down an ocean of nerves into a bone-dry throat, looking for something to say to break the silence. 'That was quite a performance. I thought you were in trouble out there,' and she gestured to the waves breaking over the harbour wall.

'Trouble?' He coughed nervously and stepped back. 'No, I wasn't in trouble. I suppose it is a bit blowy.'

Mari blinked a few times and shook her head in disbelief.

'Blowy? Right. I hope you know that you scared the living daylights out of me just now. How do you do it? How do you get into that boat and go out on the water in weather like this? I simply don't understand it.'

His reply was a twitch at the side of his mouth which told her more than a lengthy answer. Oh, yes. She had been right. The boy who had become the man was still as annoyingly arrogant and self-confident that it shone out of him like a beacon to all those around him who were still trying to find their way in the dark. And straight away she was back to being the plump, geeky girl who was the constant target of his incessant teasing.

It was so aggravating she could scream.

She was different now. She could handle this man who had become a star. They had both been so young the last time they spoke—teenagers trying to find their place in the world.

So how was it that the last time she had felt like strangling someone as badly as she did now, her client had just uploaded a virus onto the brand-new server she had just installed?

Ethan took it to the next level.

Grinding her teeth together in frustration, Mari pressed her fingers into her palms and slowly closed her eyes, then opened them while her blood pressure calmed.

'I've got used to bad weather over the past few years, and Swanhaven bay is positively calm compared to the seas in the Southern Ocean. But I'm sorry if I scared you.'

And with all of the extra confidence and self-assurance that ten years of a life spent in the spotlight and hero worship could bring, Ethan took one step closer and casually slid his left hand up and down the sleeve of her padded coat. 'Are you okay now?'

And it annoyed her so much that it sucked any chance of logical thought out of her mind, rendering her speechless. A blinking, wide-eyed creature. Just as she had been all those years ago when she'd hero-worshipped him from afar and he'd ignored her for most of the time and teased her the rest.

'You've changed your hair,' Ethan said softly, his sea-blue eyes focused on her face. He grinned the kind of white smile that would make toothpaste companies queue up to arrange sponsorship deals. 'Looks great.'

Yes, this makes my day, she thought, and found something interesting to look at on her gloves. *How dare he look even better with a few years on him? When she felt positively shop-worn and decrepit? And her hair had been squeezed under a hat for ages and must look a total mess.* For a moment she couldn't think or move. Nor trust herself to look at him again, never mind talk to him in joined up sentences.

Why did he still have this effect on her? Why? He had always had the confidence, the natural charm of the handsome, gifted people who had sailed through life on a warm breeze. And knew it. Nothing had changed in that direction.

'Thank you.' Mari cleared her throat, lifted her chin a little higher and tried to ignore her pounding heart, while forcing her mouth and head to reconnect long enough to say something intelligent when they had zero in common. 'It's been a while.'

'I was sorry to hear that your mother passed away. She was a remarkable woman,' he said in a low voice. 'I was racing solo in the Southern Ocean when it happened or I would have been there. You should know that.'

'Of course,' Mari said, desperate to take control, and managed a closed-mouth smile. 'Did you know that Rosa is still in Swanhaven these days?' She shook her head in amazement. 'She loves being here so much. So at least one of us is still in the old town.'

Before he had a chance to answer, Mari made

a point of pulling her scarf tighter so that she wouldn't have to look into those blue eyes. She was a mature woman. She could do polite to a visiting celebrity who used to be close to her family. 'What brings you here on a Friday morning in February? I thought you lived in Florida.'

'I do, but for some reason my mother has decided that she wants to retire back home in Swanhaven. So I've been building them a retirement place in the next bay,' Ethan said with the husky tone in his voice that made her very glad that she was leaning against the jetty because her knees had suddenly decided to take on the consistency of blobs of jelly. 'Dad and I designed it together but I'm here to finish the house before they move in next week.'

He was going to stay in Swanhaven for a whole week? No, no, no. How could this be happening?

Mari whipped back towards him, blinking in astonishment, and managed to link enough words together to create a sentence. 'Are you moving back here with them full-time?'

Then he smiled with his own unique, closed

lips, one-side-of-his-mouth special smile. 'That would be a no. I have a life back in Florida, thanks all the same. But I'll be around for a few weeks. Things to do. Some business to take care of. Then there is the Sailing Club.'

She swallowed hard and tried to come up with something to say but was saved when the icy wind sent another shiver across her shoulders.

'Well, good luck with that. But right now I'm freezing and I promised Rosa that I wouldn't be out long. It was nice seeing you again, Ethan. Maybe we can catch up another time?'

When Swanhaven harbour freezes over.

He turned away and started strolling away from her towards the cliff path which led towards her old home and smiled back at her over one shoulder, one eyebrow raised as he gestured towards the path.

'Looks like I just got lucky. If you're heading home I'd love to catch up with Rosa again. With a bit of luck she might find me a dry crust or two to nibble on, since I'm starving. Would that be okay?'

And then he started up the cliff path, away from Swanhaven, and straight for her former home. The home which was now up for sale. The home she was going to buy back.

He carried on walking and it took a second for her brain to process what he was doing.

He didn't know. Ethan had no clue that they had lost their home when her father left the family. But she was not going to tell him the whole bitter saga. He would soon find out for himself if he stayed around—and preferably when she had gone back to work. Rosa would tell him.

Oh, Ethan. There have been a lot of changes since the last time we spoke.

Instinctively Mari took one step forward, then stopped and called out in a loud voice, 'Sorry, Ethan, you're going the wrong way. Rosa lives in the town these days. And I hear the harbour café does a great range of snacks.'

He stopped and turned back to face her, the wind ruffling his hair into a set designer's dream of rugged and his eyebrows came together in a puzzled look. 'You sold the house? I thought your mother loved that place?'

Her breath caught in her throat as it tightened in pain. *Get it over with,* she told herself. *Just tell him and you won't have to explain yourself again.*

She looked up at Ethan, who was standing, tall and proud and so bursting with life and vitality and all she could think about was that Kit should be standing there. Her lovely, wild, adventurous brother who loved to break the rules. She had lived her early life in Kit's shadow, but she would have given anything to see him smiling back at her at that moment. Alive and well and so full of energy and potential.

Instead of which, she saw Ethan Chandler. Kit's best friend. The boy who was sailing the boat on the morning Kit went over the side and died. And it broke her heart. Worse. It broke through the veneer of suppressed anger which she had kept hidden.

'Yes, she did. Don't you know? We lost the house when my dad had his breakdown and his building firm closed down owing thousands of pounds. We haven't lived there since the summer you left. The summer Kit died. The summer we lost everything. Goodbye for now, Ethan. See you later.'

And she turned away from this god-handsome man who she had idolised as a girl and walked as fast as she could in the biting wind, back to Swanhaven and the world she had created for herself when everything around her was crumbled and destroyed.

CHAPTER THREE

'How about this one?' Mari asked as she tapped Rosa on the arm, then pointed at the laptop screen. '"Looking for a grumpy old man to nag? Try *Hire a Haggard*. Smart men aged sixty-plus. Guaranteed to last a good couple of hours if fed and watered. Dancing and friskiness at your own risk."'

Rosa put down her knitting and peered at the head and shoulders photos of older men displayed on the screen. Her face lit up with a stunned grin. 'That. Is totally perfect. I hadn't thought about renting a wrinkly. We can tell Aunt Alice that we've organised a male escort for the evening. She'll be thrilled! And at seventy-nine a man of sixty-plus has to count as a toy boy. Valentine or no Valentine.'

Mari grinned back and winked. 'I live to serve.

A toy boy! I like the sound of that. Although the idea of a male escort might come as a bit of a shock to the more snooty members of the Swanhaven Yacht Club.'

'They'll survive,' Rosa sniffed. 'Besides, we only have the Valentine's Day party once a year and Aunt Alice does manage the clubhouse. It's only right and proper that she sets a fine example to the younger generation with a dapper date. Especially when my big sister has flown all the way back to Dorset especially for the big day. This calls for posh frocks. Shoes. Bags. Plastic baubles. The full works.'

She rubbed her hands together in delight, then looked hard at Mari over the top of her spectacles. 'Unless of course you have a love slave hidden in the attic of your tiny flat, but there hasn't been much evidence of that lately. Has there?'

'Guilty as charged,' Mari replied as she shut down her laptop, 'but I have been a tad busy. As well you know.'

There was a snort before her sister answered. 'Work, work. Travel, travel. What a pitiful excuse. Anyone would think that you actually preferred living in California to coming home to Swanhaven now and again.'

Mari stared back at her open-mouthed, then tutted several times before answering her baby sister. 'Perish the thought. Why do you think I booked time out for the Valentine party this weekend?' She smiled warmly before going on but her mouth closed slightly as she murmured in a lower voice, 'I do feel guilty about leaving you here on your own to clear Mum's things after the funeral. Thank you again for helping me out this last year. It hasn't been easy.'

Rosa reached across and squeezed Mari's hand before unfolding herself from her old squishy sofa and walking the few steps across to the picture window of her terraced cottage and the view down the cobbled lane towards Swanhaven harbour.

'Aunt Alice has been making an effort to persuade me to spend more time with her at the club but things haven't been the same, have they?'

Mari shuffled off the sofa and came to stare

out of the window, her arm wrapped around her sister's shoulders. 'No,' she whispered. 'Not the same at all.' And they stood in silence, both gazing down towards the sea and the cliff path.

Directly across the lane was the parallel row of white-painted two-storey terraced houses which stretched down from the church and small primary school to the harbour and the yacht club, which served as the village meeting place. This was the temporary house which she had moved into with Rosa and their mother when they had to sell the home they adored. And here they still were, stuck.

'Do you know, it's almost ten years since we moved here? I still feel that I let her down, you know. About the house.'

Rosa turned and shook her head. 'That's ridiculous. Don't do that to yourself. She was so proud of your success and how hard you were working to make it happen. I have no doubt about that whatsoever and I was here with her every day. You did the right thing.'

'But I promised her, Rosa. I promised her that

I would do whatever it took to get the house back for us. And she never lived to see that happen. And now our old house is finally up for sale when she's not here to enjoy it.'

'I know. But we tried. We really tried.' Pain flashed across Rosa's lovely face for a split second before she beamed across at Mari. 'Of course there is one small news item that I have been keeping from you all day and the suspense is killing me. I can't hold it in a minute longer.'

There was a groan and Mari's shoulders dropped petulantly. 'Please, not another walk around the harbour looking for dogs without coats so you can sell your wares,' she whimpered. 'It's freezing out there! Jet lag. That's it. I still have jet lag.'

'Protest all you like, but I am determined to show off my talented computer guru of a sister to all and sundry.' Rosa moved closer to Mari. 'As far as this town goes, you are officially one of the local celebrities who have actually made good in the outside world.'

'Me? A celebrity?' Mari clutched the back of

the nearest chair and pretended to faint at the idea. 'I mend company servers and design tailor-made software systems, and design websites in my spare time,' she finally managed to squeak. 'That does not make me a celebrity. Believe me, the company head office is in California and the celebrity culture is alive and well.'

'What can I say? Standards here have slipped. But not for much longer. Because there is something I have to tell you.' A cunning smirk lifted one side of Rosa's mouth and she waggled her eyebrows a couple of times before taking a breath and speaking so fast that her words all ran together. 'Ethan Chandler is back in town and I really wanted you to meet him on your own at the harbour but you haven't and he is probably going to be at the club tonight so you should know about it before you get there.'

She sucked in a deep breath, chest heaving. 'There. I'm glad I finally got that out. It's been a nightmare keeping Ethan a secret for these past few days but I was so sure that you would see him around and it would all be fine. And why are you shaking your head like that?'

Mari took hold of her sister's shoulders and forced her to make eye contact.

'I saw Ethan this afternoon on the way back from my walk. He was coming into harbour in a boat smaller than your bath tub and he frightened the living daylights out of me. There. Satisfied?'

She gave Rosa's shoulders a gentle shake before dropping her hands back onto the chair. 'What were you thinking? You should have told me.'

There was a hiss as Rosa bared her teeth. 'I know, but you were always so intense when he was around. And when Kit died…you were so hard on him, Mari. And now, with all of this media interest… Stay there; I kept the article for you.'

Rosa dived back into the living room and rooted around in a basket overflowing with yarn, knitting paraphernalia, old newspapers and unopened mail until she finally found the magazine she was looking for.

She flicked through the pages, her eyebrows

tight with concentration, and then she grinned
with delight and held up the page with a thumb
and forefinger at each corner and waved it from
side to side in front of Mari's face.

Splashed across two pages of the colour supple-
ment of a national newspaper was a stunning
photograph taken of a racing yacht in full sail on
a choppy sea under hot blue skies. And standing at the helm was a tall imposing man, broad-
shouldered, tanned, with handsome features and
body language that screamed of total confidence
in what he was doing. Ethan was wearing an im-
possibly clean white T-shirt with a designer logo
on the breast, navy shorts and baseball cap. No
shoes.

His tanned sinewy legs were spread for stabil-
ity, his bright blue eyes focused on the sea in
front of him, alert and intelligent, and his arms
stretched out on the wheel. Mari scanned his left
hand for a wedding ring without even realising
what she was doing, but it was covered up with
an article praising him for his work on a charity
for disadvantaged teenagers.

'Isn't he dreamy?' Rosa was almost sighing with delight and swaying from side to side.

Mari breathed out slowly, blinked several times to break out of his hypnotic gaze, then peered at the page and almost snatched it from Rosa's hands. 'And you forgot arrogant, bossy and the bane of my life. As far as Ethan Chandler was concerned I was the nearest geeky girl with her head in a book who he could tease and torment whenever he pleased. And then ignore the rest of the time. Oh, yes, I certainly made a big impression on Ethan.'

Then she took a closer look at the date on the newspaper. 'Wait a minute. Ethan never lived here. He only came for the summer holidays with his parents. That hardly makes him a local.'

Rosa took the magazine back with a cough and smoothed out the page. 'His mother came from around here, which makes it close enough. Besides, his parents are building a retirement bungalow in the next bay and Ethan is certain to visit them now and again. That makes him a local as far as we are concerned. And the really good news is that he's back in town for a while working on his parents' house.'

Rosa paused and tapped one finger against her chin. 'The way I see it, it would be a very friendly gesture if *someone* would invite him to the Valentine's Day party at the yacht club. Just to welcome him back to Swanhaven, you understand. I would do it myself but, seeing as you had *such* a special relationship…well, it does point one way. And now where are you going?'

Mari wound one of Rosa's hand knitted scarves around her neck a couple of times before replying. 'Down to the harbour to clear my head. I've started to hallucinate. For a moment I thought I heard you suggest that I ask Ethan Chandler to the Valentine party. Which is obviously ridiculous. And no. We did not have a *special* relationship. Okay? I don't want to go there.'

Her fingers fumbled with the buttons on her cardigan and Rosa came over and fastened them for her. 'That was a long time ago, Mari.'

Mari swallowed down a denial but couldn't. 'I know. But it doesn't change the fact that Ethan

Chandler always has to win. No matter what the risks are or who gets in his way.'

Rosa smirked in reply, then tipped two fingers to her forehead. 'He always did make you frazzle. There are plenty of girls around here who think men like that are God's special gift to women on earth because we deserve treats like Ethan now and then.'

'Ethan does not make me frazzle,' Mari chortled. 'I am a goddess, and as a goddess my special power is that I am immune to handsome men. My problems are far more to do with the sixty-five e-mails which have come in since three this afternoon, and all of them are desperately urgent.'

She glanced back at the magazine and gave Rosa a faint smile and a gentle tap on the nose to wipe away the sadness in the room. 'So let's forget about Ethan and start on the really important business of planning party outfits and organising a date for Aunt Alice, shall we?'

Rosa winced and flicked a glance up at Mari. 'Drat. Um…there is one more *tiny* thing. I sort of promised Ethan that I would help him decorate his parents' house if he agreed to open the summer Sailing Regatta. And he said yes, thank you. More hot chocolate?'

Mari grabbed Rosa by the waist as she stood to go back to the jug warming on the hearth of her open fire. 'Oh, no, you don't. Sit. Do what your older sister tells you.'

Rosa faltered, but sat back down and looked at Mari sheepishly over the rim of her mug before shrugging a little as she replied. 'It seemed like such a good idea at the time. He was in town ordering building materials and hanging out at the yacht club just after he arrived. We got talking and it was pretty obvious that Ethan might be brilliant at carpentry and the like but he had no clue whatsoever about colour charts or layouts. So I sort of took pity of him and traded a week's work for two days of his time in July. His folks will be here over the summer and he's happy to have his photo taken for the TV cameras and the whole media circus. The publicity would be amazing. Swanhaven needs celebrities like Ethan more than ever. And the sailing club needs a boost.'

Mari sat back on the arm of the sofa, stunned. 'Rosa the interior designer? Well, this day is turning out to be full of surprises. I think I need to sit down.'

The doorbell sounded. 'Who can that be at this time of night in this weather?'

Mari stood to clear away the cups as Rosa chatted to someone at the door, then turned at the sound of footsteps.

'I can always make myself scarce if it's a customer or one of your new boyfriends,' she said, and turned to find herself staring into the chest of Ethan Chandler, who was grinning down at her.

Mari crossed her arms and glared at Ethan, stone-faced.

The sheer bulk of him seemed to fill all of the space in the cosy living room, and she had to fight the urge to step back into a corner so that she had room to breathe.

He was overwhelming in every way possible.

This was not helped by the fact that Rosa was peeking out at her from behind Ethan's shoulder and nodding with her head towards Ethan, flapping her face with her hand and fluttering her eyelids. Oh. Yes. Apparently she had to be polite. She could do polite.

'Hello, Ethan. Nice to see you again so soon. Is there anything that we can help you with?'

He bowed slightly. 'First, I just wanted to make sure that you got home safely. And secondly, the snow is still falling and I'm on my way to the clubhouse. Thirdly, I'm here to warn you that you may be accosted by the local TV station on your way out. So, if my favourite two ladies require an escort, personal security or a lift home, I am at your service.'

He raised his head and glanced around the room, inhaling appreciatively. 'And what is that fantastic smell? Blueberry muffins? Or cinnamon?'

Rosa groaned and rolled her eyes. 'Two. That's all I can spare. Blueberry and cinnamon. And

I do have to get to the club early so a lift would be great.'

Ethan responded by lifting the back of Rosa's hand to his lips. 'I would be delighted to have your company.'

'Oh, you are terrible.' Rosa grinned, then looked from Ethan back to Mari, then back to Ethan again, her eyes wide. 'Dress. Coat. I'll be five minutes. Maybe ten.' With a quick nod, she turned around and fled upstairs.

There was an uncomfortable silence in the room for a few seconds, broken only by the crackling of the logs in the open fire and the ticking of the old mantle clock while Mari busied herself filling a bowl with hot water and started washing the cups, aware that Ethan had strolled up to watch what she was doing, his back against the wall.

'We have to find a way through this situation somehow, Mari. And I can't do it alone. My parents are going to be regular visitors to Swanhaven, the press are in town and I will probably visit them when they are here. Can we work together to put the past behind us? Or at least agree to a truce. Any ideas would be welcome at this point.'

'A truce?' Mari laughed with a shake of the head, then sighed. 'That is quite a concept. But I do have a few questions,' she said quietly over one shoulder.

'Anything. Just shout.'

Mari took a breath and turned to face Ethan, who was looking at her with such total focus that she felt like the most important person in his world at that moment, and wanted to squirm at the same time. 'Why has the local TV station come all this way to talk to my family and neighbours, Ethan?' she asked. 'And why are your parents flying all the way here in winter when they could stay in the sunshine in Florida? Why are you really here? I don't want my sister or this community to be dragged into some part of the Ethan Chandler Reality TV show or some major marketing campaign that we don't know about. I care too much to see it ridiculed like that. And please tell me the truth.'

Ethan's arms unfolded and he pushed one hand

deep into his trouser pocket. 'Okay, I asked for that. No TV show or marketing campaign, but you are right about one thing. I've just heard that TV cameras and journalists are heading this way and are about to descend on Swanhaven. And they are all looking for exclusive interviews and feature articles.' He held up one hand. 'I did not invite them. You can blame the PR company we use for that.'

'PR company? When does a yachtsman need a PR company?'

'I frequently do,' he stated, and then his smile faded. 'But this isn't about me. It's about the sailing charity I set up just over a year ago after I got back from the Green Globe round-the-world single-handed yacht race.'

Ethan paused and licked his lips. 'I'll give you the short version. There were three captains leading the race for months. It was tight all the way. By the time we reached the Southern Ocean at the bottom of the world I was in the lead by half a day but the seas were the worst we had ever seen. Every second was a fight to stay upright.'

Mari's breath caught and she realised that she had stopped breathing.

His face was dark, eyebrows tight together. 'This was a place you don't go to unless you have to, and when you get there you stay awake for as long as it takes to get out. I still don't know what happened, but in the middle of the night I was on deck fighting a storm when my yacht hit a freak wave so hard that I went flying onto the deck. Part of my mast sheared and crashed into the cabin. I was knocked out for probably five or ten minutes and woke up with one mighty concussion and a boat that was taking in water.'

Ethan wandered over to the window, drawing back the curtains and peering down the narrow street. 'It was about as bad as I could get without sinking. And I knew it. The only good news was that my radio still worked.' His voice was softer now, as though talking to the window was easier than talking to her, but Mari could still hear the tension in his voice.

'What happened? Did the organisers launch a rescue mission?'

He nodded. 'The Australian coastguard had overall responsibility with the race organisers and they called in any commercial shipping in the area, including the other yachts in the race.'

He shook his head. 'It took six hours of some crazy sailing in which he almost damaged his boat to reach me, but my friend André was the first to arrive.' Ethan laughed low in his throat. 'I've never been so glad to see anything in my life. I managed to get into the water and across to his yacht. My boat was only fit for salvage and, by taking me onto his, André was out of the race. So we had a lot of time to talk about our lives and how we got started. We realised that both of us had learnt to sail in junior sailing clubs run by volunteers in small coastal towns like Swanhaven. It was strange, but the more time André and I spent together, the more we both came to the same conclusion. We both owed our passion for the sport to those sailing clubs.'

There was just enough change in Ethan's voice to make Mari look up and pay attention. Suddenly he sounded excited and energised. Enthusiastic.

Mari could not help but smile. 'Kit and his friends lived for that club. They did amazing work.'

'I know. I used to be so jealous that Kit lived here all year round and could sail any time he wanted. He had more freedom than I ever had back when we lived in London.'

Ethan's smile broke through the tension in the air and she blinked several times to break free from the intensity of his stunning grin.

'Did you really think that I had forgotten about Kit and the summers I spent with him here? He would have loved to run a sailing school. I know it and so do you. When I got back to Florida I took the decision to retire from competitive sailing to create a charity teaching disadvantaged teenagers to sail. I bought a huge old wooden schooner and it has taken a lot of work to fit it out as a training ship, but it's a fine vessel and does the job.'

'When did you start teaching?'

'About six months ago. The results have been amazing. The charity is turning the lives of those teenagers around. In a few weeks they can find self-confidence and skills they did not think possible. We're giving them a chance to show what they can do.'

Ethan moved closer to Mari and she leant back against the sink as he rested his hand lightly on her arm. When he spoke his voice was low and warm. 'Look, Mari, I'm here to finish the house for my parents. My mother has always loved Swanhaven. She's stayed away for ten years but this is where she wants to spend her summers. But some researcher is bound to pick up on the accident and start asking around town about what happened to Kit. And I'm sorry if they do. I really am.'

'Then you shouldn't have come back here.'

'You're right. But my mother wants to spend more time here when she retires, and I want to give something back to the town which got me started on this amazing life. That's why I agreed to give a few classes and open the regatta for

Rosa. And if that means extra publicity for the charity and the town? Then I can put up with being reminded about the accident. But what about you? Are you okay with my being here?' he asked in a low voice, and Mari shot him a sideways glance.

His head was tilted to one side and there was a look in his eyes that she had never seen before. A look which shouted out regret and concern and sorrow in one single glance, and her heart contracted so tightly she could only nod quickly in reply and turn back to her washing-up. 'I don't have a lot of choice, do I?'

His hand reached out and took hold of her wrist. 'You asked me why I came to Swanhaven, Mari. And I've told you. But if it's going to cause too much trouble or bring up too many painful memories, you just let me know and I can be out of here any time you want. As for now? Sorry about scaring you earlier. I can promise you that I will try my best to keep a low profile and try to see that Kit is not mentioned. And I always keep my promises.'

Mari looked deep into those intense blue eyes which still had the power to enthral her and was still working on a reply when Rosa skipped down the last stair with her shopping baskets, hat, scarves and gloves bundled in her arms.

'Ready when you are, Ethan.'

Ethan's mouth twisted up at one side as Mari turned to face him. 'Something tells me that this weekend is going to be one to remember. I can hardly wait.'

CHAPTER FOUR

COLD night air filled Mari's lungs as she gingerly made her way across the cold footpath to the Swanhaven Yacht Club, where the normally staid club sign had been decorated with sparkly illuminated hearts ahead of the Valentine's Day party.

Strange how it managed to be fun and stylish instead of cheap and tacky.

Unlike her shoes. She might share the same shoe size with Rosa, but she certainly would not have chosen sparkly sandals with three-inch heels to crunch through the thin layer of ice covering the snow. Rosa had taken one look at the elegant black shift dress that Mari usually wore for a casual evening and insisted that for once she should wear party shoes like a proper grown-up and she was going to choose some for her.

Fairy lights leftover from Christmas twinkled in the metal railings on the balcony of the yacht club, illuminated by the warm glow of light from the windows. As she moved closer, Mari could see people clustered around the huge log fire burning in the hearth of the old stone house. It was as though every precious, warm feeling she had ever associated with Swanhaven had come together in one place. Concentrated in one room. Inside were most of her old school friends and extended family. These were the people she had known all of her life—and in turn they knew her. Good and bad.

This was the community she had left behind—but not for much longer if her plans came true.

Almost by magic, there was a rush of movement from the entrance and Rosa stepped outside, grabbed her arm and pulled her through the door and into the hallway.

'It's freezing out there! Ethan has already started on the buffet so you'd better work fast if you want something to eat!'

There was nothing else for it but allow herself

to be dragged to the kitchen where the long pine table was groaning under the weight of enough food to feed half the town, which was probably necessary, judging by the crush of people who had squeezed themselves into the small rooms.

Mari followed Rosa past the crowds and looked around, grateful that she was tall enough to see over the heads of most of the other people there, especially in these heels.

She made her way slowly into the dining room, chatting and greeting friends and neighbours on the way, and then she saw Ethan in the small office the harbour master had once used.

And her heart let her down with a quick beat that made it pound. Palms sweaty, she gawped at the best-looking man in the room. He was wearing black trousers that had clearly been made to measure, especially around the seat. And a crisp white shirt open at the neck, designed to highlight his deep tan and the whiteness of his smile and eyes.

Oblivious to her ogling, Ethan was chatting to the chairman of the yacht club, who was standing with his arm around the shoulders of a teenage boy she did not recognise. As she watched Ethan pointing to a group photograph from one of the regattas where he had won the junior race, Mari suddenly knew exactly what she would be giving Ethan as a house-warming present for his parents. Over the years she had created a collection of personal photographs from the summers he had spent with his family in Swanhaven. She had nothing but respect for Ethan's parents and they had been totally amazing after the accident. Her mother would never have got through without their help.

The last thing she wanted was his parents to feel that she had forgotten about them or that they were unappreciated or unwelcome in the town.

And oh, the camera loved Ethan.

All she needed was a scanner to create a digital slideshow from the dozens of photographs she had taken over the years in those dreamy holidays. That way, Ethan could choose the prints he wanted from the film and have them framed! Yes! She could give them to Rosa before she left and her sister could pass them on as the final touch when she went to help Ethan decorate. And she knew exactly where the old photographs were kept in Rosa's house.

Mari gave Ethan a fleeting smile as she started to weave her way towards the bar, only to be stopped by one neighbour after another, all anxious to catch up with her news and hear all about her exciting life in computing across the ocean.

Ethan glanced over his shoulder at that moment and caught Mari smiling at him. And his breath caught in his throat so hard he could only manage a nod before turning back to chat to Henry Armstrong, the instructor who had taught Kit and himself to sail all those years ago and who was now retired and Chairman of the Swanhaven Yacht Club! When Ethan had arrived in Swanhaven, Henry had asked him if he would give his nephew Peter a few extra sailing lessons as a personal favour while he was in town. Ethan had hesitated, as his plan had been to keep a low profile. But after chatting to Peter he'd agreed to help him with some things he was struggling with.

Peter was a shy boy who held back in group lessons, but it was clear that he was passionate and talented and ready to learn. Over the past week he had grown fond of this fatherless boy who was prepared to go out on a bitterly cold day and get wet.

The only embarrassing part was how grateful Peter's mother and uncle were, and now he nodded away their thanks before watching them melt back into the crowd of friends and neighbours, some of whom Ethan recognised from the family parties he had been invited to at the Chance house when he was a teenager. Mari's aunts certainly had not changed much—they were still as eccentric as ever. Rosa was certainly cast from the same stock. But Mari? She was so different.

She certainly was not the awkward, gawky sixteen-year-old girl that he remembered.

When had Mari finally learnt to stand ramrod-straight with her head upright? What had happened to the girl who had been so cripplingly shy that she'd found it impossible to look at a boy eye to eye? And the old Mari certainly would never have had the confidence to wear a fitted dress like that! A dress designed to make best use of her stunning figure. Elegant, sophisticated and formal, it was the perfect dress for a professional woman who wanted to get the message across that she would not tolerate any form of unwelcome familiarity.

If it had not been for Kit, Mari would probably have stayed a complete mystery to him. Just another girl, who happened to be living next door to their holiday home.

And yet... Marigold Chance was the girl he *could* have asked out a thousand times, if the words had not choked in his throat each time he'd almost said them.

Ethan winced at the memory of how inadequate his best friend's younger sister used to make him feel. Mari could never be interested in him as anything more than a friend of her late brother. Why should she? Mari was a loner. Unapproachable. Contained. She didn't need to be part of a gang or play team sports to make a connection. She was happy in her own company—and he had envied her that. He had resorted to teasing her simply to get a reaction—any reaction—which meant that she took the time to notice that he existed.

What an idiot! He should have had the courage to ask her out at least once. Or at least explain that he was teasing her because he was attracted to her and was simply desperate to make her notice him.

And now Kit's sister Mari was a lovely talented woman. In an amazing dress that fitted her in all of the places guaranteed to press the right buttons in the perfect sequence. Buttons he knew he had to turn back off. And fast. And those legs!

Gorgeous and intelligent. Now that was a killer combination.

She would never forgive him for being on the boat with Kit the day he died. Just as he would never forgive himself. Each of them had found their own way to get through each day—but it never went away.

All the more reason for him to keep his distance, finish the house then get on with the work he had come here to do.

Mari shook her head in exasperation as Ethan dazzled her uncle and cousins with tales of derring-do and sailing adventures. He really did have the charm offensive down to a well-practised art and it took several minutes of manly back-slapping before Ethan glided up to Mari with her flute of champagne and his glass of cola, as though they were on the deck of a cruise ship, and started to say something.

Except that, just as she leant closer to try and hear what he was saying against the party noise, the laughter and chatter dropped away, Ethan stopped mid-sentence and looked over her shoulder in silence towards the entrance. He was white-faced with alarm, his eyebrows drawn tight together in concern and dismay.

'What is it?' she asked, concerned. 'Has something happened?'

And then Mari turned and saw why everyone had gone silent. Rosa was standing just inside the side door, her face ashen, holding her left forearm out in front of her. Her dress was covered in mud and slush and her stockings were ripped. Her hair was dripping-wet, she had lost a shoe and all in all she looked a dishevelled mess.

Mari rushed forward faster than she thought possible and grabbed hold of Rosa around the waist. 'What happened. Are you okay?'

'It's snowy. I slipped.' And then Rosa's legs collapsed under her and she slid towards the floor in an ungraceful faint as Mari tried to take her weight and failed.

It was Ethan who got there first and took Rosa in his arms before she hit the carpet, a fraction of a second before the entire crowd of people surged forward, pushing past her to help Rosa into a chair. Someone brought water. One of the lifeboat crew took a quick glance at Rosa's arm, looked back at Mari and her aunt and mouthed, *'broken wrist'*, then reached for his mobile phone to call the hospital.

A wave of nausea and dizziness hit Mari, forcing her to press her hand down on the nearest table for support. The wine. She should have eaten something before the wine. Now just the thought of food made her dizzier than ever, and she closed her eyes and fought air into her lungs.

She couldn't believe it. Only a few seconds earlier Rosa had been laughing and jigging along to the jukebox. Her aunt Alice grasped hold of Mari's arm for a second before rushing forwards from the bar to be with Rosa.

Rosa had to be okay. She just had to.

Ethan stood back, watching the scene from the back of the room, as his place at Rosa's side was taken by her family.

Rosa was surrounded by the people who loved her, while Ethan felt very much the outsider. Oh, the family were friendly and everyone here had welcomed him but, when it came to it, he was still just a visitor.

This was what he'd felt like after Kit had died. Mari had become even more withdrawn. Distant. Solitary. She had disappeared into her studies. Driven. Obsessive. Trying to take care of the family as best she could.

Mari had been sixteen going on thirty and on her own.

He had seen it and not had the skills and power to do anything about it.

How could he? His family were moving to Florida full-time, he was set for university in America and the world of sailing, and the happy summer holidays he had spent here as a boy were over for good.

Rosa had told him that Mari had decided to use her education to get out of Swanhaven. He recalled asking Rosa if she would do the same, and she'd said she'd tried, she really had, but compared to Mari? No way. Besides, she loved Swanhaven and had wanted to stay with her mother and the aunts and cousins. This was where she felt she belonged.

And then he had to leave Swanhaven and Mari and her family.

Of course everything had come to a head on the night of her sixteenth birthday party. She had waited all day for her father to turn up. But it had been Ethan who'd followed her out onto the beach and held on to her as she'd raged against the unfairness and cruelty of what he had done, talking and shouting in an explosion of suppressed emotion and crying and hanging on to him for strength until the dawn. Then he'd kissed her goodbye.

And then he had watched her pale silent face grow smaller and smaller as his family had driven out of Swanhaven. It had been one of the hardest things he had ever done. For one night he had felt an unshakeable bond with Mari which was so special. So unique. And he hadn't had the emotional tools he needed to talk to her about Kit and make her understand how truly devastated he was.

It had been easier to leave with his parents and start a new life. And he was sorry for that.

It had hurt to see her in pain then. And it hurt now.

Ignoring the other people moving towards Rosa with coats and offers of a car to the hospital,

Ethan wound his way around the room, looped his arm around Mari's waist and half carried her as far as the hall, where she had some hope of catching her breath, or at least passing out with some dignity.

She looked up at him in surprise, then, as though recognising that something in him she could trust until her dying day, she stared, white-faced, into his concerned eyes.

'The ambulance is on its way, but can you take me to the hospital to be with Rosa? Please? I don't have a car and...'

'You got it.'

As Ethan grabbed his own jacket from the hall stand and wrapped it around her shoulders, he knew it would take more than a coat to stop this precious woman from shivering. He had watched when her world had fallen apart once before, and he had been a boy. Powerless to help her, he had been forced to just stand back and watch her pain.

No longer.

She faltered on the icy steps and as he held her tighter around the waist, taking her weight, he felt her heart beating under her thin dress in the cold night air and he knew his fate was sealed.

Doomed.

In that fraction of a second it took for his arm to wrap around Mari's body, he knew that there was a chance that she could forgive him for Kit's death—a small chance, but a chance neverthe-less. And that meant more to him than he could say.

Ten years ago he had walked away from Mari without telling her how he felt about her. How could he? She had accused him of being reckless and not caring about anything but winning the race the day that Kit died. And she had been right about that. He had wanted to win. And maybe he had pushed the boat and Kit beyond what they were capable of doing, but no one could have predicted that wave hitting their boat so hard that it capsized. It had not seemed possible.

A series of unexpected events were responsible for Kit dying that day while he survived and he had relived those few minutes so many times in so many ways to know that there was not one thing that he could have done differently.

Strange how it didn't make any difference. His life had been changed forever since that morning all those years ago. And perhaps Mari was right to blame him. Because he certainly blamed himself and had gone on blaming himself, year after year, to the point when the only way he could escape the pain was by relentless action. Kit would never have the opportunity to sail in the great yacht races around the world—so he put himself through every extreme to win. For both of them.

He had run away from Mari on the morning after he had kissed her, filled with guilt and self-reproach.

Well, he wasn't running now. Mari needed him and it was obvious that she still linked him to Kit's death. It was time to make a stand.

He was making a commitment to Marigold Chance. All over again. And this time it had nothing to do with Kit and everything to do with Mari and how he felt just seeing her again.

He had his arm around Mari at precisely the time when he should be concentrating on getting back to Florida to plan the next phase of fund-raising for the charity. And the feeling was so amazing and yet so crazy and foolish that Ethan almost laughed out loud.

Her life was in computing in California. His life was in competitive sailing in Florida. In a few days he would leave Swanhaven in good hands and get back to a full workload teaching teens to sail for the next six months.

He was no good for her. All he had to do was make his heart believe it.

Mari turned over and pulled the duvet a little closer around her shoulders as she snuggled down into the cushion and gave a little sigh of content-ment.

Mmm. She had enjoyed such a sweet dream where Ethan Chandler had sat with her on this very sofa until she fell asleep. Lovely. This was such a comfy warm bed. She could lie here all day.

Her eyes creaked open and some part of her

brain registered that daylight was peeking in around the corner of the thin curtains, which looked different somehow. And it was strange that her alarm clock had not gone off. It was the last thing she checked every night without fail.

She stretched out her arm towards the bedside cabinet and her fingers scrabbled about in vain to find the clock. Her right eye opened just a little more.

It wasn't there. And her arm was covered with something pink and fluffy, which had certainly not come from her suitcase.

She pulled her arm back under the warm duvet and closed her eyes for one complete millisecond before snapping them open and sitting up in the bed.

And then collapsed back down again onto the cushions with a groan and pulled the duvet over her head.

No wonder she hadn't recognised the curtains.

This was not her cool airy apartment in California. This was Rosa's living room and she had fallen asleep on the sofa.

And Ethan had carried her inside last night because she had turned into a pathetic weeping creature the minute they had brought Rosa home from the accident department. The rest of her family had been so wonderful and encouraging while she had been totally pathetic and embarrassed herself.

She had not even managed to reach her own bedroom.

'Are you decent in there? I have coffee.'

She glanced down at her clothing before answering Ethan. She was wearing the same black dress she had put on the night before, which luckily was not creased beyond redemption, plus a long-sleeved pink sweatshirt with fluffy kittens on the front belonging to Rosa. In fact the only thing missing from her outfit were her shoes.

Yes, she was decent. And Ethan Chandler had put her to bed. And what else? She couldn't remember anything past being lowered onto the couch and someone tucking the duvet in around her. Oh! Was that part of a dream? Help!

'Coffee would be good,' was her feeble reply as

she pushed herself up on the sofa and drew the covers up to cover her chest inside the sweatshirt. Pathetic indeed.

Ethan breezed into the room carrying a tray with two steaming mugs of the most wonderful-smelling coffee and a paper bag, which he opened and presented to her as he collapsed down on the other end of the sofa, completely unfazed by the fact that she was lying on it.

The tray was made from the lid of a cardboard packing box, each coffee mug had a picture of a puppy on it and there was a marked absence of napkins or plates but, strangely, this was the kind of room service she could get used to.

'Morning. I stopped by the bakery on my way in. The lovely Rosa is awake and in her kitchen and managing quite well considering the strapping on her wrist. Apparently these are her favourite cupcakes—oh, and I found these in my truck this morning. Yours?'

He held up the pair of gold, high-heeled sandals she had borrowed from Rosa the night before, and Mari gave him a look. 'Ah, I didn't think so.

Feel free to help yourself to a takeaway breakfast. I brought enough for three.'

Mari reached inside the bag and pulled out a muffin in a bright pink paper case. It was covered in heart-shaped pink sparkles with a small blob of white icing at the centre.

Mari and Ethan both stared at the muffin for a second in silence before he laughed. 'Well, that definitely suits Rosa.'

Luckily the next cake looked like double chocolate chip and Ethan grinned and clutched it to his chest in delight. 'Your sister does have style. Coffee? The café was open.'

All Mari could manage was a single nod, and it took several delicious sips of the hot bittersweet blend before she was ready to speak. 'Oh, that is just what I needed. Perfect.'

They sat in silence for a few minutes, but it was Mari who found the courage to break the truce and say what she needed to say. One adult to another.

'Ethan.'

'Um,' he replied, between mouthfuls.

'Thanks for last night. Sorry about the crying jag. I'm…embarrassed about…well…what I must have looked like. Sorry.'

He shook his head and pursed his lips. 'You've no need to feel sorry. You only have one sister. If she hurts, you hurt. I get that. Things will look better in a few days.'

Mari gulped down a surge of emotion which threatened to overwhelm her. Ethan had come to Rosa's aid when she needed it, stayed with them when he did not have to, and now he was offering her understanding. Suddenly it all seemed too much to take in, and she covered it up by blowing on her coffee.

'Thank you. Although—' and she dared to look up at him with a thin smile '—I'm not sure if things will settle down in a few days after last night. What did the doctor say? A couple of weeks? That could be a problem for a girl who knits for a living and works in a bar.'

Ethan sipped his coffee before answering. 'Sprained wrists are a common injury in sailing and she will struggle for quite a while but things will be fine. She was lucky it wasn't broken.'

Mari dropped her head to focus on folding the muffin paper into tighter and tighter V-shaped angles. 'I almost feel guilty about leaving so soon when she needs help—but I must get back to work next week.'

'She knows that you came a long way to spend time with her. In the snow. And you even had to put up with me for a few hours. That's quite a sacrifice. Your sister is going to be fine.' And he reached for his second muffin.

'Hey!'

'What? I missed my dinner too. And breakfast. Did you know it's almost ten?'

'What?' Mari gasped, almost spraying coffee all over the duvet.

'Relax. You were exhausted. Sometimes it pays to let your body have a rest. I'll go and check on your sister. And try to wake up.'

Mari looked up just in time for her face to be inches away from Ethan's middle, as he lifted his left arm above his head and stretched it out towards the polystyrene ceiling tiles, rolling his shoulder to shrug off a mighty yawn. And she almost dropped her drink.

Tight, perfect six-pack. Deep tanned abs. No muffin-top hanging over the top of these jeans. A faint line of dark hair ran down between the bands of muscle below his belly button and, as he stretched up to grasp both hands behind his head, she noticed a touch of silky elastic waistband. Silk boxers. Navy check.

He still smelt wonderful.

Only now that outdoor, aromatic cologne was mixed with something else. Sweat. Plus something unique to Ethan she had almost forgotten about.

Oh, yeah. Ethan smell.

Starched white shirts and shoe polish.

She used to make a point of sitting as close to him as she could manage without being a stalker, just so she could smell his laundry. Her own clothes had never seen an iron, because they did not actually own one that worked, and every surface in their house was usually covered in a mixture of cat hair and sometimes paint and linseed oil splatters.

He stopped moving.

She kept staring.

He just smiled and brushed the crumbs from his fingers onto the tray.

Mari moistened her lower lip with her tongue. 'Ethan. One question. Did you put me to bed last night? That was you, wasn't it?'

She watched him slip off the sofa and head for the door, only to turn at the last minute and grin.

'Maybe. Maybe not.' And he dived out.

'How can you still look fabulous with your wrist all strapped up like that? It is so totally unfair.'

Rosa kissed Mari on the forehead and waggled her elbow before wincing a little. 'It's a burden I shall have to get used to. The pretty scarf helps. And the painkillers are really most excellent. I feel quite giddy. Remind me not to drink any wine tonight or there'll be more contorts…tortoises…sprains to go with this one.'

'Oh, I will.' Mari smiled and sat down next to

her sister at the dining room table. 'You are not leaving this house today, young lady, that's for sure.'

'Bossy boots,' Rosa hissed at Mari, then sat back in her chair and grinned at Ethan, who was just finishing off his second breakfast of cheese on toast washed down with scalding-hot tea. 'I bet you wouldn't make me stay inside for days, lovely man. Would you?'

Mari lifted her eyebrows and stole a sly glance towards Ethan, daring him to side with Rosa before he replied. 'You are grounded, young lady. Better get used to it. The last thing my house needs is a crazy one-armed girl going mad with a paint sprayer.'

Rosa groaned and dropped her head onto her outstretched right arm. 'Oh, no. The decorating. What are you going to do? I'm so sorry. I forgot. What still needs to be done?'

'The building work is done. Utilities, water, the lot.' He raised his right hand. 'I still need to finish the decorating and the final detail with the furniture and textiles. Everything that's going to encourage my dad to finally take a rest and retire while he's still fit enough to enjoy life. And there is the small matter of the fact that I promised my mum that the house would be ready when they get here next weekend.'

He dropped both elbows back to the table, clasped his hands together, lifted his chin and stared at Mari, his eyes never leaving her face as he spoke. 'I already called three decorating firms and they're booked solid until the end of February. I need help now.'

There was a stunned silence in the room, broken only by the crackling of the logs in the open fire. Then Rosa blew out a whistle and waved her bandaged wrist towards Ethan.

'Ethan, I can't do much except give directions. Unless...' Then she pushed herself slowly off her chair, slid around the table so that she was sitting next to Ethan, and leant her elbows on the table and gave him a conspiratorial wink.

As though they had rehearsed their movements in advance, Ethan and Rosa lowered their chins onto their cupped right hands in perfect coordination and both of them just sat there, staring into Mari's face.

'Your mother was the best home decorator this town has ever seen.' Ethan paused and added in a low, calm, matter-of-fact voice, 'I already have the paint and supplies Rosa recommended, and the house is full of stuff. What I don't have is an extra pair of hands and someone to make it all come together. If *only* someone would volunteer to take Rosa's place and help me out, it would make all the difference to my parents.'

Mari realised what was happening and held out both hands palm-forward in denial.

'Oh, no. Don't even go there! I'm here for one long weekend, and then I have to get back to work next week. There's no way I can take on a big decorating job in two days. There is also the small matter of my total lack of artistic talent. Computers. I like computers…and two against one is totally unfair.'

Rosa smiled sweetly at Mari before speaking. 'This is your time to shine, Mari. And don't give us excuses about your lack of talent. You were always the better artist at school—and everyone in the family agrees that you are totally brilliant at photography.'

'Family! Great idea. Why don't we call the cousins?' Mari gushed as she felt the ground slipping away from under her feet. 'Maybe they can take time away from work for a couple of hours? And I'm sure one or two of them can hold a paintbrush!'

Rosa gasped at Mari. 'If you like black! Aunt Lucy's twins are into Goth and are both at college at the moment.' She paused. 'Of course, both of Aunt Alice's sons are colour-blind, but they would help! There could be a few spare minutes between shifts behind the bar at the club.' Rosa's voice faded away as she shrugged towards Mari, who dropped her head to the table and knocked it a couple of times on the cloth.

Mari sat back and looked from her sister to Ethan and back to Rosa again, closed her eyes for a second, then shook her head before sinking back into her chair in resignation. 'Yes. Okay. I will do it. I will help you decorate your house.

But under protest. I don't like emotional blackmail.'

'Understood, but thank you, Mari, all the same. In that case, I'll pick up the supplies we need and be back here in about an hour,' Ethan replied, leaping up to go before anyone changed their mind, but he could not resist turning back and giving her a warm smile. 'No time like the present. And who knows—by the end of the day, you might even enjoy it!'

Ethan ducked as a half-eaten muffin came flying towards his head. Only the plan backfired as he caught the cake one-handed, stood back up and took a huge bite. 'Mmm. Not bad. Not bad at all. Any more for the workers?' And then he dived out of the door before Mari could find something harder with more bounce potential.

Leaving the two girls looking at one another in silence.

'What?' Rosa asked in all innocence. 'You want to work behind the bar at the yacht club all day? No, I didn't think so.'

She glanced at her watch. 'Better get some

rest, because it sounds like you're going to need it, Mari. Put the cake knife down, Mari. I am wounded, remember? Ouch!'

CHAPTER FIVE

THE snow had stopped during the night, leaving a crystal-clear blue sky morning.

Mari stared out of the window of Ethan's four-wheel drive, peering through the thick pine trees and mixed forest to the inlet before they reached the shore.

The branches of the low fir trees had been painted silver and white by the heavy frost and looked like something from a Christmas card. She should have brought a camera and made some greeting cards for Rosa, like she used to when she was younger. Rosa would love that.

Great. More guilt. Just what she needed.

'You've gone quiet on me again. Is this so terrible? It's a nice day. The sun's shining. The snow has stopped. Want to give me a hand unloading the car?'

She looked at him, shook her head. 'You really hate to take no for an answer, don't you? And using my own sister to help you decorate! Shame on you.'

'For what?' Ethan replied, raising both hands away from the steering wheel for a fraction of a second. 'I was telling you the truth! I need the help. It's that simple. And who else am I going to ask? Your mum was a goddess in home decoration and you did more than help. I was there, remember? Lugging cans of paint and wallpaper all over the county in your dad's old van. You can't fool me, Mari. I saw you in action too many times. Who knows? It could be fun.'

He glanced over at her just before she turned away to gaze out of the window.

Or maybe not.

'Did Rosa tell you about the house? We have three bedrooms en suite. Air con. Triple glazing. And the best view this side of the bay with a private jetty.'

'Didn't there used to be a cottage down that way?'

Ethan nodded. 'A derelict fisherman's shack.

The planning authority didn't want the land used for a hotel on the protected seafront. And it was too far out of town for a restaurant or the like. So when it came on the market, I bought it with permission to rebuild that one house on the shore. Plenty of other people wanted to develop the site and build a private housing complex and offered a whole load of money for the privilege. But I outbid them. This is where my mother wants to retire to, so this is what she gets. And here we are.'

Whatever mental picture Mari had created of a house by the shore, she was totally unprepared for the image she found at the front of the house. They had driven through a single break in the tree cover onto a paved driveway, leading to one of the most stunning buildings she had ever seen in her life.

The house itself was one storey, hugging the shoreline, with an attic floor above, the peak of the tiled roof just low enough so that the pine trees on either side still towered above it.

But that was not the killer. It was the view.

The house was not just near the sea. It was on the shore. From the drive, she could see the long glass panels of a conservatory built on stone pillars extended a few feet over the water. To her right, the drive continued down to what looked like a solid wooden boathouse, the roof heavy with snow. On the left a double door garage below a curving extension, which seemed to fit seamlessly into the forest. The cold air was filled with a wonderful combination of pine needles, sawdust and a tang from the choppy ocean which spread out in front of them to the other side of the bay.

Ignoring the fact that Ethan had started unloading his car, Mari walked towards the boathouse so she could get a clear view across the water to the snow-covered hills. A low line of housing on the other side of the shore and the town of Swanhaven was hidden by the angle of sight.

It was a different world. Magical, private and serene.

And totally stunning.

Ethan came up and stood by her side in silence,

his hands stuffed into his jeans' pockets as the icy sea breeze buffeted their faces.

They stood only inches apart until Mari shivered. She looked at Ethan and said in a calm voice, 'You win. It's fabulous. Now I understand why your folks are willing to leave Florida for a few months every year.'

The silence opened a gap between them. Their smiles locked.

And just for a fraction of a second Mari allowed herself to relax and enjoy being with Ethan as an attractive man who had been her first kiss all those years ago, and the feeling shocked her so badly that she was the first to look away.

She covered up her discomfort by rubbing her hands together for warmth. The sooner she got on with the job, the sooner she could be out of here and back in town to take care of Rosa. 'Okay. Let's do this. Show me what you need help with.'

'Come right this way. I have three rooms with bare plaster. Three large rooms. And paint. Lots of paint. Then they need fittings and furnishings. Rugs, curtains, cushions. Everything.'

Mari whistled. 'I see what you mean. We had better get started then.'

Ethan leant forward very carefully and peered around the corner of the lounge towards Mari to make sure he did not disturb her. Kit's little sister was wearing an old, navy, extra-large boiler suit and a pair of sailing boot socks to protect the fine wooden floor as she cleaned and polished, and at that moment he thought she looked just fine.

As he spied on her, Mari started to sing along to some tune or other she had in her head like she used to do when she was happy. He had forgotten about that. Forgotten how comforting it was to have Mari around. Simply being in the same house and the same room.

Of course he would never admit it, but sometimes he missed being part of the Chance family show. Kit had been the eldest child—the gifted and special boy. The apple of his parents' eyes and a true sportsman, like his dad. But Rosa and

Mari were the characters, the deep and interesting people who kept their dreams and their ideas inside and preferred home or study to getting soaked in Swanhaven harbour at every opportunity, like Kit.

They might have had the same parents, but he could not imagine meeting three more different teenagers. And things were never organised or boring in the Chance house.

Rosa was always the soft-hearted charmer who was almost incapable of offending or upsetting anyone. An artist like their mother; like her, she appeared to have no ambition or drive to be anything other than what she was—they were completely happy to live their lives in Swanhaven. He envied Rosa that serenity. She certainly was totally different from Kit, who'd excelled in pushing the boundaries on a daily basis.

As for Mari?

On the surface, the Marigold Chance he was looking at now was very different from the geeky, self-conscious girl who had been the star pupil in high school compared to Kit, who'd adored her just the same. Back then her long hair had been as wild and uncontrollable as her sister Rosa's. Now the glorious, glossy, curly auburn hair had been tamed into a straight shoulder-length style, so that her fringe just covered the dark curves of her eyebrows.

Last evening at the club she had looked a lot more polished and confident. A lot taller than her five feet eight inches. He had watched her chat with old friends and relatives but, at the same time, he could not help but notice how she still drifted away into a corner unless one of her family was around. Mari may have changed on the outside, but he could still see the girl he had known, who liked to stay in the background, watching other people. Usually on the other side of a camera lens.

Perhaps that was why he had been so shocked at the transformation when Rosa hurt herself and the fear and deep emotion that she was capable of peeked out from her slick outer persona?

That could explain why he had sought out any opportunity to be in physical contact with her the previous evening. Helping her out of the club, into and out of his car, holding her next to him in the hospital waiting room and then hunting out a bed cover so that he could cuddle it around her on the sofa.

He was pathetic! But it had meant that he could really look at Mari close up.

There was a crease in her forehead, which showed her years of work and stress. No doubt the Swanhaven gossip network would update him with each and every achievement and promotion, but to him it was all there, written in that face.

That so very beautiful face. The pale skin. Untouched by sunshine or make-up. Plain. Natural. Cold. She might be living in California, but this girl wasn't spending her time in the sun.

The pain in his chest, which had winded him at the shock of seeing her again out of the blue, meant that it almost hurt to look at her.

Mari was still a girl living inside her head. Contained. His best friend's clever sister. The girl who had tried so hard to take over the reins when her brother drowned in a freak sailing accident and their father deserted them. He knew that in her eyes she had failed and her little family had been torn apart in pain and grief.

The ghosts of the past still ruled the closed interior world where Marigold Chance spent her life. Those dark days were still there, acting as a barrier between them.

And there was no getting away from that—they could not go back to the people they had been as teenagers. And maybe he didn't want to.

His life was in Florida. Not a small coastal town in Dorset. It had been his decision to launch the sailing school in Florida. Now he had to prove that André and the charity could rely on him to stay the course. And that was precisely what he was going to do. The faster he could finish the house and get back to his new life, the better.

Mari and Ethan lay on the floor of the conservatory, with their bodies stretched out in opposite directions. Both of their heads were resting on the same small lounger cushion so that Mari could just feel Ethan's head move as he looked around. Dusk had fallen over the shore outside the window and the light fittings were still bare wires hanging loosely from the ceiling.

Ethan shuffled his jeans-clad bottom on the thick cream tiles Mari had just spent an hour buffing to a lustrous shine. 'This truly is the best way to test that the under-floor heating is working properly. Seriously. Temperature sensors are just not the same.'

'I shall have to take your word for that—but it does sort of make sense. Radiators would look totally out of place in here.' Mari raised her head towards the ceiling. 'This is a truly excellent viewing position.'

She dropped her head back so that she could just feel the contact with his short-cropped hair, and looked up to the slanting clear glass roof of the conservatory. Snow had slid from the special glass and most of the clouds had been blown away during the past hour to reveal patches of sky, already twinkling with stars. There was no moon, and the constellations were clear and sharp, as though newly painted.

'Come here often?' Mari asked, chewing the inside of her mouth to block the smile in her voice. 'Or do you bring all of your lady friends here to impress them with the view?'

Ethan chuckled. 'This is the first chance I've had to actually enjoy the place. The wooden floor went down three weeks ago. I only had a weekend to get the job done, then I had to get across to see André and finalise our sailing project plans for the rest of the year. Busy, busy.'

'Ethan the carpenter. This is going to take some time for me to get used to. Tell me about southern Florida. What made you stay there?'

'Accident. Serendipity if you like. My first major sponsor ran an upmarket hotel and apartment complex on the coast, and I just loved it down there. Climate. Lifestyle. The whole package. And plenty of work. The world-class yachting fraternity love Miami and the Caribbean. Add in the small fact that my dad has built an amazing architectural firm back in his home town and suddenly Florida ticks all of the right boxes.'

'Ah. Does that mean you had a lot more to prove?'

Ethan's answer was a low chuckle that made the floorboards vibrate beneath them. 'Oh, yes. Still working on that one. Although I think he still hasn't totally recovered from the shock of me actually offering to stay in one place long enough to teach sailing. How about you? Silicon Valley I can understand, but you could work anywhere. Why stay in California?'

'I actually went to Los Angeles because of a boy, but California has everything I need. There's a lot going on at the moment, which is why I'm flying back on Tuesday.'

Ethan swung his legs up and turned around so that he was facing Mari.

'Whoa. Hold it right there. You. The famous No Chance girl, moved to a city because of a boy? This I have to hear about.'

She shrugged. 'There you go, jumping to the wrong conclusions. I never said I was there for romance, did I? The boy in question was a place-ment student at the IT company I worked for in

Swanchester who casually mentioned that he had been invited to a recruitment interview with a major Silicon Valley firm, but he was on his way to cancel. He had already accepted another offer closer to home.'

'What happened?'

'I sweet-talked my way into taking his place, had a great interview and got the job. Right place, right time. And I've been there ever since.'

'Hmm. Funny how things happen. Great opportunities love to just fall out of the sky. Would I know the name of the firm?'

Mari reached into the back pocket of her trousers with much squirming and passed Ethan a creased and slightly warm business card.

He gave a low whistle. 'You weren't kidding. My dad has used this company. Not bad for a girl from Swanhaven. Not bad at all.'

'Why, thank you, kind sir,' Mari replied in her best Californian accent. 'The surfing dudes just love my cute accent on the telephone.'

She fluffed up her hair, and then remembered that the estate agent was supposed to be e-mailing her after 4:00 p.m. to confirm the time for the house auction. 'Speaking of which, I suppose I should be getting back. I need to check my messages.'

'Surf dude?' And he made a sliding motion with his hands. 'Is some hunky youth polishing his board until you get back? Seeing as you are so cute.'

Mari rolled her eyes. 'Strictly business. Let's just say I'm between boyfriends at the moment.'

His smile faded. 'Seriously?'

'Work is crazy. The company pays me to respond to other people's emergencies. That's my job, and I do it very well, but it's a killer for any kind of social life. I did have a long-term boyfriend, if you must know, but businesses need software in a crisis and he eventually got fed up with me cancelling on him at the last minute. It's as simple as that. Could you do your work without internet or e-mail or computer technology?'

'No, I couldn't. But that sounds like a pathetic excuse to me. Damn shame. But I suppose you are right. Speaking of cancelling at the last minute,'

Ethan hooted as he pulled on his shoes, 'have you seen what time it is? At some point this morning I foolishly promised Rosa that I would have you home in plenty of time for the no doubt delicious dinner your aunt has cooked. And you've done your share today.'

Mari sat up from the hard floor at the same time as he did and grasped his outstretched hand to pull herself up. And kept hold of it.

Both of them knew where any conversation about boyfriends was going. They were adults.

'And what about you, Ethan? Do you have a lovely girlfriend waiting for you back in Florida, or is it more of a case of a girl in every port?'

Her tone was fast and jokey, only Ethan still had her hand in his and started to run the pad of his thumb up and down the centre of her palm and wrist, his eyes locked on to her. Mari sensed his breath quickening. His palms were getting sweaty.

'As a matter of fact, I don't have a lady in my life at the moment,' Ethan replied, taking her question seriously. 'Long sea voyages don't do much for relationships and I know how hard it is for the sailors to say goodbye to their loved ones. And it's a nightmare for those left on the shore. Competitive sailing is a selfish and dangerous sport.' He shrugged, then he smiled that lopsided smile that made her feel giddy. 'A bit like rally driving on snow. Ready to take the risk?'

CHAPTER SIX

THIS was just a ride home from an old friend of her brother's.

It had started to snow heavily soon after they had arrived and the roads were now covered with several inches of compacted snow and ice.

No big deal. *All she had to do was trust him.*

There was silence. She stared out of the side window, aware that they were both reflected against the dark night. Ethan glanced across at her.

'I don't like it when you go quiet, Mari. What's the problem?'

She paused, and then turned to look at him.

'I was just thinking back to all the times you argued black was white that you would hate to stay in one place for more than a few weeks. And now you're teaching in Florida. Wow. You've had

such an amazing sailing career and well, that is…
quite a change in direction.'

He sniffed and shrugged his shoulders. 'I was
at the top of my game. Best time to walk away.'

'It's still a brave decision.'

He turned off the main road and started onto
the unlit tarmac before speaking, the windscreen
wipers moving slowly to clear the light snow,
which was still falling.

'Maybe. And how about you, Mari? What's
brought you from sunny California this weekend?'

He glanced across and scanned her body, from
her scuffed boots to fleece jacket. 'Not that I'm
complaining, you understand. Looking good.'
And he winked before focusing on the road.

She couldn't help but grin back. 'You noticed,'
she said, and pulled her jacket tighter around her
shoulders. 'This time I flew in from Denver. But,
to answer your question, I was working all over
the Christmas holiday so I promised Rosa that
I would pop back to celebrate Valentine's Day.
I have some business in the town, and then I'm

on the last flight from London on Tuesday. And that's it. Short visit, but that's all I can squeeze into the diary at the moment.'

There was a snort from the driver and Mari turned in her seat to stare at Ethan as he shook his head in disbelief.

He slapped both hands hard against the steering wheel, making Mari jump.

'How could I forget the Valentine's Day party? What an idiot. That's the day after tomorrow, isn't it?'

Mari looked at him in disbelief and chuckled out loud. 'You forgot? How could you forget Valentine's Day? It must be serious.'

'I've been working on a completely new sailing course back in Florida. The idea is to take a whole crew of troubled teenagers on a voyage lasting a couple of weeks. A sort of summer camp on water. It will take the next few months to set up and finance and the admin is horrendous. I thought racing was busy until I started this project.'

He glanced at her quickly before going on. 'The

sailing side I can handle and my parents are helping with the project management. But there is a lot at stake here, and scoping out the project is taking a lot longer than I expected.'

He stopped talking, and Mari frowned. 'Ethan, I can hear the cogs clunking inside your brain from where I'm sitting. And there's a strange burning smell. Out with it.'

'I was just thinking how great it would be if some computer guru created a totally flash website for us that would totally sell the project to sponsors. And it would have to be free. Any idea where I could find a specialist like that around here? Mari?'

And he glanced across at her with the kind of smile designed to make old girls blush and young girls squeal.

Mari couldn't help it. She put her head back and laughed out loud.

'Thank you, but no. You should be ashamed. There are brilliant PR companies who do charity work for projects like yours. Go and find one!'

'Oh, there has to be something I can do for

you as a trade? Here's an idea. In return for a few days pro bono work, I shall be delighted to escort you to the Valentine party tomorrow and defend you from the amorous clutches of the half dozen single men still left in Swanhaven. What do you say? Do we have a deal?'

Mari sat open-mouthed for a few seconds, her eyebrows high. 'Are you asking me to go with you as your date? Or a paid escort service? That is disgraceful. The old Mari might have done it but not this new girl. See you at the party.'

She paused for a second and gestured at the window towards the cottages down in the village beneath them. 'I've changed, Ethan. When are you going to understand that?'

'I don't think you've changed that much,' he whispered eventually, and gave her a small smile. 'Not where it matters.'

'Well,' she answered, 'it's good to know that the great Ethan Chandler can be wrong about some things. There is hope for humanity.'

That made him laugh, and it was so contagious she smiled back in return. And something flickered between them as his eyes briefly met hers. Something that made her want to get out of this car as soon as she possibly could.

Chemistry. Chemistry as bright and as spectacular as a meteor shower.

Instead of which, she turned her head away and pretended to focus on the buildings either side of the main road into the town.

Her eyes blinked several times as she tried to clear her head. And persuade her heart to slow down before they reached Rosa's cottage.

Focus. That was the key. She needed to focus on why she was here.

She had forgotten how dark it could be on the country roads without streetlights. Occasional drifts of snow lifted up on the open fields on one side of the road but she knew that on the other side was the shoreline and the long pebble and sand beach which led down to the sea. It seemed to take only minutes for Ethan to drive the few miles to the brow of the hill she knew so well.

She reached up with her left hand in an old familiar gesture and clasped her seat belt, ready for the long descent into the bay and the stone harbour that led into Swanhaven, but instead the car slowed and Ethan pulled into the viewing spot on top of the hill where tourists could take photographs of the picturesque fishing harbour below them. She could almost visualise the curve of the old stone harbour wall, the new marina with the pretty sailing boats and the ocean beyond stretching out to the horizon.

He turned the car so that they could look down onto the lights of the town below and make out the curvature of the bay. Mooring lights in the tops of the yacht masts in the marina twinkled in the cold, crisp, clean air. They had left the snow clouds behind them and stars were shining bright in a deep black freezing sky. It felt as though they were on top of the world looking down from the heavens like some strange Greek gods.

Mari released her seat belt and shuffled forward so that she could rest her chin on the back of her hands on the dashboard and look out over the view.

And all the time her body was hyper-aware that

Ethan was sitting only inches away from her, his strong arms outstretched on the steering wheel. Every inch of her skin prickled with being so close to him, and she could feel their connection growing tighter and tighter.

Oh, no. She was not going there again. She still felt guilty about kissing Ethan the last time. She *had* to change the subject and break this silence. She just had to.

'I do have something up my sleeve which might cheer my sister up. I'm planning to move back to Swanhaven for good.'

'Move back?' Ethan's voice was low and deep and resonated around the car. 'Wait a minute. Why didn't you mention this earlier? Rosa didn't say a thing!'

'That's because my lovely sister doesn't know anything about it. So please don't breathe a word about it or I will never be forgiven.'

The crease lines at the corners of Ethan's mouth lifted, white against tanned skin and afternoon stubble. 'Okay. Your secret's safe; I owe you for this work. But why are you keeping this to your-self? She'd be thrilled to know that you're even thinking of coming back.'

'Okay,' she replied, flicking her tongue out over her lips, and something in Ethan's gut turned over and kept spinning like plates on a stick. 'You remember the house we used to live in, the house on the shore on the other side of town?'

'Of course. I loved that house. We had to walk past it every day from the place we rented. I'll never forget that amazing mural your mum painted on your bathroom wall. All blue, covered with tropical fish, wasn't it?'

Mari chuckled out loud. 'Rosa painted sea horses, and I just about managed a Picasso ver-sion of a starfish. It was amazing. I miss that house. A lot.'

Ethan noticed that the corners of Mari's eyes were glistening as she spoke but she gave a brave smile.

'Hey! You'll make a home for yourself like that one day. Give yourself time,' he murmured, sud-denly wanting to reassure her.

'You're right. I could buy a cottage in the town like Rosa's, except for one thing. I don't want a house *like* that one. That's not good enough. I want *that* house. My old home. And I mean to get it.'

Ethan kept on rubbing his thumbs up and down the base of the steering wheel, but something was badly wrong as he looked into her eyes and he dropped his hands onto his knees as she went on. 'Did you know it was up for sale? Well, guess what? I'm going to buy it. I'm going to buy my old home back.'

Both of her hands clutched Ethan's arm now, her face bright with energy and excitement, her body jazzed to the point of jumping around in her seat.

'Isn't that the craziest thing you've ever heard of? I've worked every hour and every vacation I could to raise the money, but I've done it. I've saved enough to make a respectable offer for the house and land at the public auction and the bank is giving me the rest. Don't you see? I have a chance to move back here and live with Rosa in our old house. What do you think of that?'

Ethan slid back in his seat against the car door, swallowing hard.

'Well? Say something!' she said and shook her head at him.

'I guess I'm just a little confused here. I thought that you had made a new career for yourself away from Swanhaven. I mean, your old house? I haven't seen the place, but I should imagine that it would cost you serious money to make it a home again.'

She nodded furiously in reply. 'I know. I've worked the numbers. It will take time and money to restore the place and update it so I can run an online IT business from the house. I'm thinking four years at most. Maybe three if I get the Denver contract and sell my place in California and stay in my job long enough. The company are laying off technical staff but I have to hope for the best. And in the meantime Rosa could live there and work her decorating magic.'

Ethan breathed in through his nose. *What was*

she thinking? Her company was laying off staff and she wanted to buy a house in a pretty tourist area close to the beach.

A cold feeling developed in the pit of his stomach. She was setting herself up for bitter disappointment.

'I'm sorry to hear about the job worries. Land prices have shot up around here over the last two years. You could be outbid. What are you going to do then?'

'That's why I didn't tell Rosa,' she answered in a low voice tinged with sadness. 'She was so traumatised when we lost that house. If I am outbid?' She inhaled sharply. 'It would be hard. I don't even know if I could handle that disappointment. But Rosa would be destroyed all over again. It would be like losing it twice. I couldn't do that to her, Ethan, I just couldn't. But I can't think that way. Because I'm not going to lose that house again. Three years, Ethan. Three years from now I can be living in my own lovely home again. And in the meantime Rosa has a house which nobody can take away from her. This is

our security for the future. That's why I'm determined to win that auction tomorrow morning.'

'Tomorrow? That's cutting it fine. I thought
that you were leaving on Tuesday.'

'I am. But it's all going to be fine. I've already
organised the legal side and Rosa and the family
can look after the details.' She paused and tilted
her head to look at him. 'What is it? You look
worried.'

He blew out a long breath, misty in the cold
damp air, and took hold of both of her hands and
pressed them against his chest.

'Moving back here could be a mistake, Mari.
A big mistake.'

Mari blinked several times as the impact of
what he was saying hit home. 'Mistake?' she said,
hardly believing what she had just heard. 'What
are you talking about? I vowed the day we had
to move out that somehow I would find a way to
get that house back. And this is the first chance
in ten years. Isn't it worth trying?'

He squeezed her hands tighter together. 'Of
course. But I wonder if you've really thought this

through. Things are so very different. Everything has changed.'

Mari gulped down a sense of dread at the chilly tone of Ethan's voice.

'What do you mean?' she whispered.

'Let's say your offer was accepted,' Ethan replied, and this time his voice was calmer and more reassuring. 'And you bought back the house your dad built for his family. Rosa would still be living in town and working at the club and you would be working every hour in California to find the money to pay the bills—if you had a job. And all that time the house would stay empty and unheated and deteriorating while you tried to find builders and tradesmen who could repair ten years' worth of neglect before you could even think about designing improvements. It would be a nightmare of stress, Mari. Is that what you want?'

'I thought you would be happy for me,' she murmured, her eyes locked on his.

He smiled sadly. 'I do want you to be happy. But your old loving and happy home is gone,

Mari. Kit is gone. Your mum is gone. Your dad is gone. And Rosa has her own life and a job she loves. Have you even asked her if she wants to move back into that house? I'm sorry, but all I can see is a lot of pain and disappointment.'

'What?' Mari pulled her hands away and slid back and away from Ethan.

'Look, I didn't mean to upset you. I mean…' Ethan paused and dropped his head back.

'Oh, do carry on,' Mari said in a hoarse whisper, trying not to sound too bitter or angry and knowing that she was failing miserably. 'Why stop now when you're so bursting with good advice for other people? I would hate to hold you back.'

There were a few seconds where all Mari could hear was Ethan shifting on the leather seat but, when he answered, his words rang out clearly in the small space that seemed to have suddenly become even smaller around them.

'This is coming out wrong, What I meant to say was that it sounds like you're going backwards in your life. I don't understand why you would want to lock yourself away in that old house with Rosa and all of the ghosts from your past and throw away the key.'

Mari's eyes sparked ominously. 'Well, I'm glad to say that you are totally mistaken, Ethan. About me, about Rosa and, most of all, you're totally wrong about what we're going to do with our lives.' Her words were coming in fast, angry, loud bursts and she reached out and slapped her hand down hard on her seat. 'How dare you? How dare you tell me how to live my life? Perhaps you should take a look at how well you have been doing these past ten years.'

'I've been doing just fine, thank you.' He nodded, his brow furrowed.

She lifted her chin. 'Have you? All those fine trophies for doing the one thing you seem to excel at. Running away. Or is that sailing away? Take your pick. Because it's all the same to me. When was the last time you came here? Oh, yes. Just before you ran out on me and left me to clean up all of the mess that you left behind in my life. No.'

Ethan had moved forward to try and comfort her—but she pushed both hands palm-forward and turned to stare out of the car window at the view.

'After everything we've been through together, I actually thought that you would understand why I want this house for Rosa. Well, it looks like I was wrong. Very wrong. It looks like we've both changed more than you know.'

She sensed his movement and turned her head towards him.

'Mari,' he said in exactly the same voice she had always known, only deeper and more intense than ever, and she looked up into his face. 'I'm sorry. I understand more than you can know.'

In that second their eyes met and any lingering thoughts she might have had that she could stay away from Ethan and walk away from this town without having her heart broken flew out of the window and into the cold night air.

And, almost as if he was feeling the same thing, his arm slipped away from the steering wheel and both his hands reached up to cup her chin so that the thumbs could swirl gentle circles on her cheeks.

Time slowed to a dead stop so that her entire senses were focused on Ethan's breathing and the warm scent of him filling the tiny space that separated them.

With one small shift in his seat, Ethan closed the space between them and his lips touched hers, warm and strong and tasting of all her forgotten hopes and dreams. All of her buried emotions surged back into life as if they had never been away but had kept dormant, waiting for this moment. And her heart swelled with such an overwhelming combination of anguish and love that when she pulled back she was afraid to open her eyes in case this was all some mirage, a dream.

'It seems that some things haven't changed at all. Have they?' Ethan said, his mouth half pressed against her temple.

'Yes, they have,' she replied in a low and trembling voice, her eyes focused on his shirt as she fought to remember how to breathe again. 'I've changed my mind. I won't be helping you out at the house after all. I quit.'

The auction house was already half-full when Ethan sauntered in and found a seat at the back of the room. Curiosity about Mari had won out in the end and he quickly spotted her sitting in the front row.

She had brushed her shoulder-length auburn hair into a shiny straight column held back by a single barrette. The stiff formal look was completed by a dark grey skirt suit and, from what he could see from this position, the same dark laptop bag she had been carrying everywhere. So this was what she looked like when she was in business mode. Impressive.

The ugly duckling of a girl he had once known truly had become a swan.

Beautiful to look at, serene and calm, and pedalling like mad under the water where nobody could see how desperate she was.

Oh, Mari. You're better than this cold, impassive creature of your own making.

Yesterday he had seen glimpses of the girl he used to know when the real Mari slipped out from beneath the weight of the past and the huge unspoken barrier that lay between them.

And it was magical.

So why did she truly want to buy back the house where she used to live with her family? He remembered it well. The house itself was fairly basic, with a stunning view over the bay from its position on the cliffs, but he had never truly paid much attention to the house. It was the family who'd lived there that was remarkable, and Marigold Chance had been the real star of the Chance home. He had never understood why he seemed to be the only person who saw that.

The auction room was filling up now and people were starting to block his view, so Ethan quickly moved forwards and took a seat directly behind Mari where she could not see him—but he could see her.

He could see how her shoulders stiffened and lifted a little when the auctioneer arrived and took his place at the podium. There was still twenty minutes to go before the start of the auction, but she was already tense and nervous.

There was the faintest whiff of the same perfume that she had been wearing yesterday in the air, mingled with heat and moisture from cold, damp clothing and a dusty room. Ethan sat back in his chair, but just at that moment the lady next to him dropped her handbag and the contents spilled out around him.

And Mari turned around to see what the commotion was, and saw him. He didn't know who was more shocked. But her wide-eyed astonishment said it all.

She stared at him through narrowed eyes, shook her head from side to side just once, checked her watch and picked up her bag, leaving her coat on the chair to reserve her place, and then tipped her head towards the entrance.

He got the message. And followed her outside.

'Are you stalking me? Because I have to tell you that one kiss last night does not entitle you to follow me around. And don't you dare try to interfere in this auction.'

Then Mari stopped, pressed her forefinger to her chin and took a short intake of breath before Ethan had a chance to answer. 'Oh. Oh, silly of me. I forgot. Why should you? I'm the one who's planning to stay in one place long enough to make a home. But you wouldn't know about that, would you?'

'Are you quite finished?' Ethan asked in a calm quiet voice as he leant with his back against his car.

'No, actually I'm not. But I only have a few minutes before the auction starts and it's freezing and you get me all frazzled when I'm trying to be calm and in control. So please. Just tell me. Why are you here?'

Ethan pushed both hands down into his trouser pockets and steadied himself.

'Good question. Long answer. Let's start with the stalking.' He raised an eyebrow. 'Someone clearly has a very high opinion of themselves.' Ethan did not react to Mari's instant cough of dismissal but carried on. 'But you have a point. I am here to see you. I'm here to see just how far you are prepared to go to move right back to where you were ten years ago.'

There was a sharp intake of breath from the woman standing in front of him with her arms crossed before she answered with a look of total disbelief on her face. 'You know why. I'm buying this house for my sister. She needs a secure home. And...' Mari stretched out her neck a little. 'It's an excellent base where I can create business at some future point. Do you have any further questions or can we go inside now?'

'Only one. How long are you planning to keep that excuse up? Because, the way I see it, you aren't buying this house for Rosa—you're buying it for yourself.' He pushed himself off the car and reached out and fought off her protests to wrap his sheepskin coat around her shoulders.

He pulled the front of the coat towards him, with her inside. 'You can fight me all you like, but I just hate to think that you're going to come back here to lock yourself away from other people. Oh,

I know. People can leave, people can hurt your feelings and people can break your heart, but sometimes it is worth taking the risk.' His voice dropped even lower and he gave a half smile as he smoothed down the front of his coat.

'You don't need to be so afraid. You can live anywhere you want and go anywhere you want. And you'll be fine.'

She looked up at him and her jaw tightened. Her eyebrows came together but she forced them apart and licked her lips before answering. 'This is all I know. This is what I want.' And she quietly slipped off his coat and strode, head up, back into the auction room.

Oh, Mari. I do hope that you know what you are doing.

The first three properties seemed to take forever to sell and there had been several breaks in the bidding when Mari had felt like screaming. Didn't they know that she had been dreaming about this moment for years, and been awake half the night worrying and the other half reliving the moment when Ethan had kissed her in the car?

How dared he turn up this morning and ruin her day with all of his questions? How dared he kiss her and give her a glimpse of all of the things she could not have? He was leaving, she was staying and he *still* kissed her. Worse. She had liked it. Stupid girl.

Either way, she was exhausted, her hands were shaking in anxiety. And the bidding was just about to start.

She didn't know whether to be sick into her laptop bag, stand on the chair and scream at everyone that this house was *hers* and they'd better not even think about bidding, or calmly sit there and make her bid at the right time.

She went for option three.

Her real worry was the size of the deposit she had to put together before the bank would agree to offer her a loan for the maximum she could afford on her salary. The constraints meant that she had a working budget with enough left over to do the repairs and create a home office. And that was all she had. Anything else would mean going back to the bank for a bigger loan, and they had not exactly been impressed by her proposal in the first place.

Without the extra cash deposit from her over-time and all of her cash savings, she could be in trouble.

And the prices so far had been a lot higher than she had expected.

But of course that would not happen with her. The photographs and house details had made it clear that a lot of work was needed. That was bound to drive down prices.

Right. Mari lifted her chin. Three. Two. One. Go. She was about to buy back her home.

Ethan clutched tight hold of the back of the chair in front of him, two rows behind Mari, his fingers wrapped around the hard metal rungs, knuckles white with pressure.

As the auction started, he felt himself being caught up in the electricity and excitement. Bids were flying everywhere from all corners of the room so quickly that it was hard to keep up. The numbers were higher than he had expected, which could be a problem. But Mari was calm. Her head fixed in place. Waiting. Waiting for the perfect time to place her bid to buy back her old home and start a new life. Back where she'd started.

And there it was. Mari raised her hand and bid a startling amount of money for her old home. But there was one more bid. From a middle-aged man at his side of the room, sitting next to a woman and three children, each of them almost bouncing with excitement and enthusiasm. A family wanted the house.

Ethan's heart sank. If he was in that position, with his wife and children around him, all looking forward to a new home by the sea—he would move heaven and earth to make it happen.

And without warning an icy chill hit Ethan hard in the stomach with such speed and ferocity that he had to take several long breaths to calm his thumping heart.

She was going to lose this house and it would

destroy her. It would be better in the long-term if she made a future somewhere else, he believed that now, but it would still cause her huge pain if she thought that she had let Rosa down.

Mari immediately raised her hand again and increased her bid by another ten thousand—and was instantly outbid again.

She was so startled that it took her a full second to recognise that the family man had increased his bid by not ten thousand but another twenty thousand.

The astonishment and alarm on Mari's face said it all. She clearly had not expected to pay anything like this much and Ethan recognised by the telltale way she chewed her lower lip and bent her fingers into the centre of her palms that she knew she was at her limit.

She hesitated, her hand almost shaking, before increasing her bid yet again.

And the longer Ethan watched Mari, the more he thought that this was not the action of a woman looking for a home back in Swanhaven with her sister. This was a desperate act driven by a need to come back to the security of the past life she had once known.

The life which he had played a part in destroying.

And he knew exactly how that felt.

Because, sitting here amongst these strangers in a dusty, cold auction room, it was as obvious as a slap in the face that he was no different from Mari whatsoever.

Watching Mari struggling with her decision at that very moment, the answer screamed out at him from Mari's startled hazel green eyes. He *was* running away from the pain and the guilt that was Kit and Mari Chance and everything that happened in Swanhaven ten years earlier. It had been easier to leave and not come back and start over again in Florida with his father's new job, and he did feel guilty about that—his whole family had—but they had made the decision and acted on it. While Mari had stayed trapped right here.

It was ironic that he should only realise that fact when he was right back *in* Swanhaven. Looking at Mari. Who had stood up and was winding her way towards him, her face lined and grey and tense with concern. The weight of disappointed dreams hung heavy on her sagging shoulders.

Part of him was pleased. Her agony was over. Now she could start moving forwards, not backwards. And perhaps give him a few tips on how to do that along the way. He started to get up, ready to take her home.

Only she grasped his arm in a powerful grip, leant forwards and pressed her mouth close to his ear. 'I need another forty thousand. Will you lend me the money? Please. I'm desperate. If you don't lend me this money I will lose the house. This is my dream. This is what I want more than anything else in the world. Please help me.'

Ethan shifted his body back just far enough to look into her eyes. And saw such terror of the unknown and a deep-seated pain and anguish in that one single look that his heart broke all over again.

His actions had helped to bring her to this place.

Now he had to be strong enough to risk the fragile bond that had grown between them. Because giving her his reply was one of the hardest things that he had ever had to do. It was wrong in every way. But he had to do it. To make Mari's dream come true.

'Yes, Mari. I will lend you the money. As much as you need.'

CHAPTER SEVEN

'WELL, it looked to me like you'd been crying ten minutes ago when Ethan dropped you off. That's all I'm saying. *Crying.* Okay? So where did you go this morning?' And then Rosa gasped and pulled her chair closer to the table. 'Of course. I should have realised. Ethan kidnapped you and whisked you off for a romantic date somewhere. That has to be it. That is *so* totally brilliant. Now, tell me everything.'

Mari sank lower into her chair at the cottage and admitted defeat for the second time that day. Once Rosa was determined to discover something, there was no point in fighting her. She would find out eventually. Half of Swanhaven had been at the auction, out of curiosity if not to bid, and the small-town gossip factory was alive and well in the yacht club. It would be around the whole town in an hour that Marigold Chance had just bought the old Chance house for twenty per cent above the expected value.

She was going to have to tell Rosa. And soon. All she had to do was pick her moment.

'I spent the morning with Ethan at the property auction in Swanchester and—' Mari took another sip of tea and considered making up an elaborate tale of love and debauchery but she simply did not have the strength to go along with anything but the truth '—Ethan and I had a bit of an argument. But in the end, he helped me out. In fact, you might almost say that he came to my rescue.'

'Ethan Chandler came to your rescue. At a property auction. Right. Well, that makes total sense. One minute you're all over him and this wonderful house he's built for his parents, and the next minute you're crying over your baked beans on toast.'

Mari hugged her tea close to her chest and stared out of the window.

Rosa bristled and gestured towards the door. 'Ethan's probably down at the harbour giving

Peter Morris his sailing lesson. I can march down there in two minutes and find out what happened for myself if you don't tell me right now.'

She sighed dramatically and waved a piece of toast in the air. 'Of course it would make a terrible scene and half the town would be on the dock in a flash, but nobody upsets my sister and gets away with it. You just give the word and…'

'Stop right there. Yes, Ethan didn't upset me. He just…' Mari shook her head and bared her teeth '…has this amazing talent for doing something totally unexpected and getting me all worked up in the process.'

'Nothing new about that. And did I mention that I wanted details?'

Mari looked up at Rosa. This was it. This was the wonderful moment she had been looking forward to when she finally, finally, told her baby sister that their dream had come true.

'If you must know—' she grinned '—I asked him to loan me some money so that I could buy a house this morning. In Swanhaven.'

Rosa collapsed into a chair, mouth open.

Mari nodded, and took Rosa's hand between both of hers. 'Yup. It's all true. I set my heart on a particular house, I didn't have enough, so Ethan loaned me the extra I needed to make the winning bid.'

And that shut her sister up for all of ten seconds before Rosa asked quietly, wide-eyed and incredulous, 'Are you really telling me that you have bought a house in Swanhaven?'

Mari nodded and tried not to look elated, but a bubble of happiness was welling up inside her and threatened to burst out in the form of spontaneous laughter. They might even be dancing.

'Not just any house. Our house. The beach house where we grew up and were so happy together as a family. I've been planning it for months, Rosa, but I didn't want to tell you in case I got your hopes up for nothing.'

Mari was almost bouncing with excitement, her shoulders practically jiggling as all the nervous anticipation and excitement of that morning came flooding out. 'I came so very close to losing it and if it hadn't been for Ethan I would have. I made a bit of a fool of myself by doing the one thing I promised myself I wouldn't do. I bid everything I had. Only it still wasn't enough. But I did it, Rosa. I finally did it. We have our house back. Isn't it wonderful?'

Rosa slipped her hand out from between Mari's and took in a sharp breath between her teeth. 'Oh, Mari…what a mess. I was going to tell you tomorrow, but now I'm sorry I waited.'

Rosa started pacing back and forth across the kitchen, pulling one cookery book out and then putting it back on the shelf before picking up another and all the time carefully avoiding looking at her sister.

As Mari watched Rosa, a growing sense of concern slowly, slowly, pricked at her bubble of happiness and the longer she watched, the more her sense of happy excitement faded with it. 'What is it? I thought you would be totally thrilled. This is what we both want. Isn't it?'

Rosa stopped pacing, turned back to face Mari and took a firm hold of the back of the dining room chair before speaking but, far from being thrilled, the tone of her voice was sad and filled with regret.

'Do you remember taking all of those photos of my scarf collection last autumn?' she asked. 'I talked to each customer who came into the newsagent's to model a different scarf for me? Well, it was a bit more successful than I had expected.'

Mari smiled into her sister's face before replying. 'Let me guess. You have to knit like crazy for a bulk order for some fancy shop. That's wonderful. We're going to have all of the studio space you need at the house.'

Rosa held up her unstrapped hand. 'Please let me finish. This is hard to say so I need to get it all out in one go. It's more than an order, Mari. One of the customers runs a handcraft design centre in an expensive part of London. She got in touch through the website a few weeks ago. There are workshops, design studios, everything. And she asked me to manage the craft shop for her, Mari. Full-time.'

Mari looked up into the face of her sister, unable to speak.

'I said yes, Mari. I want this job—it's so perfect I could have designed it myself. I'm going up to London next week to make sure that it is everything she claims. But if it is? I plan to move to London straight away. And I don't know when I'll be coming back.'

Mari's mouth fell open in shock.

'What? Rosa! You can't be serious. I thought you loved Swanhaven.'

'I do—and I probably always will,' Rosa replied, clutching at Mari. 'But this is my dream job, Mari. Crafts are my passion and the thought of working with them full-time makes me so excited that I can hardly believe it. I did the research ages ago but there was no way I could afford to take three years out of my life to study textiles in a city like London. It's way too expensive. This way, I can work, study and have somewhere to live.'

Rosa's eyes implored Mari to understand. 'You were the person who told me that I should grab on to any chance for happiness I could find—and this is it. This is my chance to show people what I am capable of. If I don't take this job now I'll regret it for the rest of my life, Mari.'

'But you don't need to move to London now. You could work at the house, build your business and sell on the internet. It would be fantastic.'

'Yes, I could.' Rosa nodded, her mouth thin and sad. 'But I don't want to. For once in my life I want to do something different. I want to go to London and find out about the craft business. I want to go to college and learn from the best. And I'm not going to do all of that in Swanhaven. I'm so sorry, Mari, but you really should have involved me in your plans.'

'Wow,' Mari breathed and sat back. 'You're serious about this, aren't you? But what about our dream of moving back to our old house? I thought you wanted that more than anything. Are you going to give up on that so easily?'

Rosa shrugged. 'You're right. I did want to move back when Mum was still with us, but that's all changed now. Have you been up to our old house recently?'

Mari shook her head before replying in a low voice. 'Not for a couple of years. It hurt too much. Oh—I know it needs work. The house details made that quite clear, but we could restore it together. Just the two of us. It would be great.'

'No. It would not be great.' Rosa shook her head, then lifted her arms and let them fall down. 'This is a total disaster, Mari! I cannot believe that you didn't ask me before you bought that old wreck of a house, expecting us to live in it. It's a shambles, and I certainly don't want it.'

'How can you say that? That was our home!'

'No, Mari. It's a house that used to be our home.' Rosa looked around and waved her good wrist. 'This is my home—at least for another few weeks! And then I'm leaving to start a new life and new future. And it is not in Swanhaven.'

Then her voice softened as she flicked Mari's hair behind her ear. 'Oh, sis. What have you done? Was this for me? Yes? Oh, Mari, I love you, you know that, and you are my one and only sister, but I don't need a babysitter any more. I'm looking forward, Mari, not back. It hurts me to think that you can't do the same.'

'What? Have you not been listening? We could make this house work, we could make it like our home used to be…' Mari started to form the words to tell her all about her wonderful plans for buying their old home back and that Rosa did not have to move to London at all.

Rosa could stay here. And be with her and live the life…she had imagined for them both.

And suddenly the selfishness and stupidity of that idea jumped up and bit Mari hard on the ankle. There was no work in Swanhaven. Rosa was right. There was nothing for Rosa here but more of the same things that she had been doing with her life so far. She'd thought that her sister was happy and fulfilled here, *and she'd been wrong.*

Staying here would mean that Rosa might never find another way to fulfil her own dreams and potential. And that was just too sad to think about.

Rosa was able to find happiness living somewhere else. Living her passion.

Mari swallowed down tears and blinked hard to cover up her distress. 'Well, it looks like I have to get used to the fact that my baby sister is all grown-up with ideas of her own. It's come as a bit of a shock.'

Her reward was a one-armed hug and a kiss on the top of her head. 'I'll leave you to work out what you're going to do with this house you've just bought,' Rosa said, then laughed out loud. 'Marigold Chance is back in town. That has to be worth celebrating. See you later.'

Mari managed a small wave in the vague direction of her sister's back. 'Later.'

Perhaps coming back to Swanhaven for the Valentine Day party had not been such a good idea after all. *She could hardly wait to find out what more wonderful news the rest of the day would bring.*

The pale winter afternoon sunshine was trying to break through the clouds as Mari strolled down the narrow cobbled street towards the harbour and the yacht club.

The annual Valentine party had always been a special time in Swanhaven and, judging by the street banners, bunting and displays in the shop windows, this year was going to be no exception.

It was almost like old times, Mari thought as she turned the corner from the yacht club onto the quay. Then suddenly stopped, mesmerised by what she was looking at.

An old wooden sailing ship was moored in the harbour. It was a single-masted traditional brig with a lovely wooden hull and decking, which must have docked that morning. She could have looked at the stately and gorgeous ship all day, like many of the locals on the quayside who had gathered around to admire the brig.

But that was not the only cause of her fascination.

Mari stared in amazement at the man who was kneeling on the deck of the ship, holding a thick rope in one hand and showing a teenager how to form a special knot with the free end of the rope. The boy was gazing in rapt attention at the complicated knot that Ethan was showing him for a second time, and looked so much like Kit at that age that Mari's heart contracted.

But it was not Kit. It was a boy in a bright yellow life jacket who was so intent on twisting the rope into this special knot against a piece of rigging that when he had finished and stood back, it was Ethan who laughed out loud and broke the tension.

'You must have been practising, Peter. My arms are getting tired just holding on! Ready to test it yet?'

His question was met with enthusiastic nodding from the boy, who stretched out far enough to tug hard on the rope several times to make sure that it was firmly attached. 'All done, Captain,' he said with a jaunty salute to Ethan, who sat back on his heels to salute back.

'Well done, first mate. Stand at ease.'

Ethan was back on his feet in seconds, but not before he had slapped the boy firmly on the back and given him a warm hug across his shoulders.

But it was Ethan's face that Mari was focusing on.

And what she saw on that smiling, happy face

hit her squarely on the jaw and sent her spinning. The intense pleasure, the happiness, his own delight in bringing such joy to the child, was reflected in that open-mouthed grin for all to see.

Ethan would make a wonderful father.

How had she not seen it before?

He wanted to show his *own* children how to tie ropes on a ship and how to sail. And he wanted it so badly it hurt her just to see it on his face and know that he had no idea how open and totally exposed that need was for all to see—or was she the only one to see it?

Any child with a father like Ethan would be a very lucky child indeed.

What a shame that he would never have the chance to settle down and be a father with the life he led.

Well, she would know about that.

Over the years she had often thought about having children of her own, but she had always kept that dream carefully locked away inside a stout box labeled: Later. *When I'm back living in Swanhaven in my old home. That's when my life will start and I can be happy. That is when I can think about children and a family of my own. And maybe even a husband to go with them.*

And in a flash the true impact of those ideas jumped up and slapped her firmly across the back of the head.

Wake up! She had done it! She had actually done it! She had bought back her home.

She had signed the paperwork in a daze and knew that it would be days before the legal documents were ready to be processed and money had to be transferred, but this was it.

Telling Rosa was one thing. But seeing Ethan working with this young man? The true impact of what she had done—no, what *they* had done, hit home and hit her hard.

Suddenly everything was different. She felt as though a huge door to a secret chamber had been opened and all of the dreams and goals she had kept hidden for ten years were suddenly exposed to the light and released from their captivity.

And a family was one of them.

She had chosen to put her personal happiness and her dreams of having her own children on hold, and now—now she didn't have to. She had just bought a huge family house which would be heaven for any child.

Of course she would be living there on her own, alone on the cliff, trying to create an online business, so meeting men could be a bit of a problem. But she could do it. Couldn't she?

Perhaps there was still time for a relationship—she was only twenty-six. She could make an effort if she was ready to change. If she was prepared to take the risk.

Perhaps that was why she'd always made sure that *she* was the one who broke up with any man who dated her more than a couple of times, because that way *they* never had a chance to break up with *her*. The truth was, she had driven her last long-term boyfriend away because she was not ready to open up her emotions and heart and let him into her life.

Mari looked up just as a pretty woman in a long woollen coat walked along the jetty to the

brig and the boy practically flew off the deck towards her. They looked so much alike that there
could be no doubt at all whose son he was, and
the woman wrapped her arms around her son's
shoulder before twisting around to face Ethan.

'How is Peter getting on? Almost ready to go
out on his own?'

'Mum!' Mari heard Peter reply, but it was Ethan
who smiled reassuringly. 'Not there yet. We have
a couple more sessions before the main season
starts. Right?'

The teenager just grinned back, his face full of
hero worship.

Well, she couldn't blame him for that.

The memory of Ethan's hands on her body, his
mouth on hers, only the evening before, had her
heart racing just to look at him.

As for Ethan? Maybe he was right. Maybe the
life of a competitive sailor was too selfish and
way too hard for the people they left behind. But
surely the good times would make up for the time
apart?

Mari watched Peter and his mother stroll further down the jetty towards a smart little boat with a distinctive red sail. Leaving Ethan alone on the brig.

Deep breath. Had she really asked him for money? Then cried with happiness all the way back to town in his car? That was so embarrassing. He must think her even more of a fool than he had before.

So why was it that something in the back of her mind told her that she might kid some of the people some of the time but, when it came to it, she just couldn't kid herself?

His kiss last night in the car had been so annoying precisely because it had given her hope that there could be something between them after all of these years.

But, in the cold light of a February afternoon, the gulf in their choices was only too clear to see.

He was going back to Florida and a life of sun and sea.

While she had just bought a house in Swanhaven and she would have to work every hour of every day for years to come just to pay off her debts.

There was no future in a relationship between them.

It was time to leave before either of them said or did something that could not be unsaid or undone. Something that would make one of them choose to change their lives. And she was way too scared by the emotional turmoil that had been building up inside her since the moment she'd seen him sail up to the jetty to have any hope of logical thought or rational decision-making.

He would be here until the end of the week and she had so much to organise with the house before she flew back to California. She simply didn't have the time for distractions like Ethan Chandler. No time at all. She had things to do. People to see. Some photographs to scan. And only a few more hours to do it.

In the meantime, nobody had warned her that having her dream finally come true after so long would be so bewildering that she felt giddy just at the thought of everything she had to do and the life ahead of her.

She needed to talk to Ethan. His father was an architect. He would know the next steps she needed to take to make her new home safe and sound.

As for Rosa's little bombshell?

Her shoulders slumped. He had been right about Rosa.

So. Time to pull on her big-girl pants and go and eat humble pie.

She needed Ethan's help. *Again.*

Ethan had just thanked the captain of the brig when he noticed Mari strolling along the jetty towards him. She had changed out of her suit into more casual trousers and fashion boots below a light jacket and smart scarf. Her hair was loose around her shoulders, her laptop bag slung over one shoulder and she looked every bit like the tourist she most surely was.

Gorgeous, infuriating, stubborn, irrational and

absolutely lovely. His palms were sweating and his mouth went dry just at the sight of her.

He had been quiet in the car on the short journey from Swanchester back to Swanhaven for one simple reason. She had been crying every single second of the way. The intensity of the tension inside the car had been in such contrast to the almost friendly attitude and sense of connection of the previous evening that he almost regretted agreeing to the loan.

Almost. He had made the right decision—this was what Mari wanted. He knew that. But it didn't make it any easier when, deep inside, he could not shake off the fear that this girl was setting herself up for a life of lonely isolation with only the ghosts of the past for company. She was going to have to work hard to create a secure future for herself, but she was strong enough to make it happen. Even if she had to pay a high price for living here.

Perhaps it had been a mistake to offer her the money—but the Mari he was looking at now was not a girl who had lost her centre, but a lovely adult woman who knew what she wanted and was determined to get it, even if it had meant waiting all of these years.

He admired her for that. And there was the added advantage that they were locked together now by bonds more than the past. He was part of her present and her future. No interest. Just connection. Good enough.

And at the very least she had stopped crying.

Smiling to himself and more than a little curious about what she needed, Ethan walked slowly away from the town along the jetty towards his boat and waited for her to catch up.

'Mari, I hope that you're feeling better now,' he managed to whisper, and then coughed to cover up how nervous he felt.

'Much. Thank you.' Mari looked around and nodded towards Peter, who had slipped onto the boat and was practising with his sails as his mother looked on. 'So he's one of your students?' she asked.

Okay. She was making an effort to break the ice after the crying. The least he could do was go along with it. 'Peter's uncle was one of my instructors and when he found out I was in town he asked me if I could help Peter with a few coaching sessions as a personal favour. I wasn't too keen but actually it's been great. Peter is a shy boy who doesn't do well in groups but he has talent. He'll be fine.'

He turned back to face Mari and tipped her chin up so that he could see her eyes. 'And what about you, Mari? Are you fine? You had a busy morning. Buying a huge family house is an exhausting business.' *Are we fine?*

Mari shrugged. 'It certainly is. I've just told Rosa the good news.'

Ethan nodded and winked. 'Well, that explains the smile on your face. She must think it's Christmas morning in her cottage. I suspect elaborate celebrations are now being planned.'

Mari sucked in a breath to calm her nerves before speaking in a voice which emerged as a long sigh. 'Not exactly. Rosa and I had a long overdue chat just now and it turns out that she's planning to leave the town for a new job in London.'

Mari flashed him a glance when he half snorted in surprise. 'Yes, I know. Looks like I was wrong.' She licked her lips and pushed her shoulders back. 'In fact, it seems that I've been wrong about quite a few things. Starting with the fact that she doesn't want to stay in Swanhaven, and she certainly doesn't want to live in our old home with me. How about that?'

Ethan stared into Mari's face. She was trying to be brave. When the one thing she had been working towards for so long had turned out to be a damp squib instead of a glorious rocket display. She was holding it together better than he had thought possible.

And his admiration and respect just went up a notch.

'That must be hard when you've taken care of Rosa for so long. But I suppose she has to make her own decisions. You should be proud of giving her the courage to want to lead her own life. It won't be easy.'

Mari had been playing with the strap on her bag but, as he spoke, she looked up and her face brightened. 'I hadn't looked at it like that. Thanks. You're right. She should lead her own life. And she'll always be home for the holidays.'

'Absolutely. So you'll be living there on your own?' he asked and, when she gave a way too fast nod, he simply smiled. 'Well, in that case, I'd better ask my dad if he could design you a fine-looking IT studio. Home office, big glass windows overlooking the sea. Oh, yes, that would be something.'

His reward was a closed-mouth smile. 'Yes, it would. But perhaps I should start with plumbing and electricity? In fact, do you mind if I pick your brains about the repair work?'

'No problem, but phone calls may be needed.' He paused and got busy with the rope holding his boat to the jetty. 'Speaking of which, I'm going to need your bank details to transfer the money. Just drop me an e-mail. That would be fine.'

Mari stepped closer towards him so that, even

on the empty jetty, only he could hear what she said next.

'That's why I've come to apologise, Ethan. I should never have put you in that position this morning. I am sorry. You were more than generous. I thanked you then, but thank you. Really, I don't know what I would have done if you hadn't been there. And if you're still looking for help at your parents' house I would be happy to get involved. If you want me to.'

She was looking at him now, almost hopeful.

And something very close to excitement and happiness hit Ethan hard. This was turning out to be quite a day.

'Well, in that case, we'd better get started, but there's one slight change of plan. My car is back at the house. I came in by boat.' And he looked at her and then tipped his head towards the sailing boat bobbing on the water, then back to her again.

Mari sniffed and crossed her arms. 'Oh, that is so cruel. You know why I've not been on a boat that small for a very long time.'

Ethan nodded slowly. 'If you want me to accept your apology you're going to have to get into that boat. It'll take ten minutes to get back to the house. Come on, Mari. Let's get this over with. Look, I will even start the outboard motor. Now that's some dispensation.'

Her arms slowly uncrossed and she started to speak, then looked into his boat in silence and bit her lower lip.

'I can't, Ethan. I just can't. I can't get into that boat. I can take a taxi.'

Mari. He watched her walk as calmly away from him as she could, down the jetty towards the beach and the cliff road, her head down against the wind, shoulders high inside her jacket making her look thin, small and fragile and almost child-like in so many ways.

Well, that had been a mistake! And he was a fool for even suggesting it.

She had been so happy this morning and in an instant he had wiped all of that joy away.

What had he told Mari? That she would be making a mistake in coming to Swanhaven? How ironic. He was the one who had made the mistake coming back here. He should have let his father complete the house in his own way and stayed where he was until the redevelopment project was complete.

That way he would not have met Mari again. He would not have talked to her, laughed and joked with her, worked by her side, and he certainly would not have made a connection.

Ethan slapped his hand palm-down on the side of his boat, hard enough to make him wince with pain.

Stupid! He should have known that coming back here would reopen old wounds and feelings that he had thought long dealt with. Especially now Mari had bought back the wreck that had been her old house and wanted to make some kind of home there.

Mari.

Ethan quickly wiped down his hands and shrugged back into his jacket.

Time was up. He strolled casually down the jetty to where Mari was standing, frozen, staring out across the bay, facing away from the ocean and peering up onto the cliff-top where Ethan knew her old home was.

She had wrapped her arms around her body as though trying to warm herself and block out the bone-penetrating icy wind, now flicked with faint sleet.

He walked slowly over, unfastened his own sheepskin jacket and stepped behind her, so that he could reach out and wrap the warm jacket around her body, pressing his shirt front against her back, his arms crossed in front of her coat so that she was totally enclosed inside his embrace.

Neither of them spoke as Ethan followed her gaze out to the dots of light which were flicking up on the far shore, his head pressed against her hood.

He closed his eyes. There had to be five layers of clothing between their skins, and the freezing wind howled around his bare hands. And yet… He was holding Mari Chance in his arms and it felt so right. So very right that it was madness.

Slowly, slowly, he dropped his hands to her

waist, cuddling against her, and started to turn her around to face him.

As though awakening from a dream, Mari realised that she was not alone and her head twisted towards him inside the huge coat. As her body turned slowly, his hands shifted so that when her chin pressed against the front of his shirt, his arms were now around her back, pressing her forwards.

His eyes closed as he listened to her breathing, her head buried into his body, protected from the icy wind and the sound of the waves lapping against the stones on the shore.

Her arms, which had been trapped inside his coat, moved to wrap around his waist so that she could hold him closer.

A faint smile cracked Ethan's face. She was hugging him back. Taking his warmth and devotion.

He dared not risk taking it any further. Dared not break that taste of trust she was offering him.

Hugging her tighter, Ethan dropped his face a

little so that his lips were in the vicinity of her forehead.

Mari responded immediately and looked up as he moved back just far enough so that he could see her face under the hood.

Their eyes locked. It was a moment in time. But, just for that single moment, everything that had gone before meant nothing. They were a man and a woman who cared for one another very deeply, holding each other.

It seemed the most natural thing in the world for Ethan to run his lips across her upturned forehead, then her closed eyes, her breath hot against his cheek. He felt her mouth move against his neck. Stunned with the shock of the sensation, he almost moved away, but paused and pressed his face closer to hers, his arms tight on her back, willing his feelings to pass through his open hands, through the clothing to the core of her body.

This was unreal.

A single faint beam of light streamed out from the lively harbour that was Swanhaven in the early dusk and caught on Mari's face like a spotlight in the gloom of the dock. The faint golden light warmed her skin. They were both cold, but there was no way Ethan would break this precious moment when the barriers were down and he could express what words would fail to convey.

His hands slid up and down her back. His mouth moved across her cheek, and he felt her lift her chin. Waiting for his kiss. The kiss that could warm that frozen centre her deep loss had created.

Adrenaline surged through his body, his senses alive to the stunning woman he was holding in his arms, his heart racing. He could feel her warm breath as they looked into each other's eyes, both of them open-mouthed. Nose almost touching nose. His head tilted. Ready.

Ethan opened his eyes to look into the hazel-green eyes of this remarkable woman who he felt he had known all of his life. His dream was about to become a reality.

CHAPTER EIGHT

SUDDENLY, out of the corner of his eye, Ethan saw something on the bay.

It was a sail. A small boat with a red sail with a black symbol on it.

It was Peter's boat, and he could just make out a small figure standing at the tiller, turning the boat into the wind so it sped across the water, faster and faster. Too fast. Way too fast. And he was on his own. Almost at the same time, he caught a glimpse of Peter's mother running towards the yacht club for help.

Ethan jerked back, his hands pulled away from Mari and he frantically grabbed her hand and half dragged, half pulled her back to the jetty and physically lifted her onto the boat without asking permission or forgiveness.

It took precious seconds for Ethan to untie the

rope, start the engine and rev it to maximum speed so their small craft bobbed violently against the waves as it raced towards the red sail.

'Ethan, what is it? Please. You're frightening me. Tell me what's happening!'

'It's Peter. That boy I've been teaching to sail these past few days. He's out in the bay on his own and something's gone wrong. Look! The red sail!'

Every time he took his eyes off the water to look at Mari in the fading light, all he could see was a small huddled figure with her eyes closed, clinging on to the side of the boat. Teeth gritted, flinching with every wave that struck the boat side-on.

Then out of the still night there was a shout, then the unmistakable sound of a human body crashing into water.

Then silence. Absolute silence.

Peter's boat was stationary, listing to one side. And there was no sign of the boy.

Ethan slowed the engine and coasted a good distance from the sailing boat and, just as they got close enough to see what was happening, the boat came to a juddering halt which made Mari scream out in alarm.

Ethan scrabbled over the side to see what they had hit, then took a gentle but firm hold of Mari's arm. 'It's okay. It's a piece of wood. A tree trunk. It's just below the water level. We're not damaged. But Peter is not in the boat. I need you to take the tiller for a while. Please.'

Mari looked terrified but, with a silent nod, she carefully made her way to the back of the boat and took control.

Ethan frantically fought to get his balance at the side as he looked back and forth along the waves for any sign of the boy, calling his name louder and louder. 'Peter! It's Ethan. Peter!'

'There! In the water! Ethan!'

Ethan whipped around. Mari was pointing into the waves a few yards ahead of the boat where there was a splash of red in the surf.

Without a moment's hesitation, Ethan stripped off his boots and dived into the freezing waves, the shock of the cold paralysing him for a few seconds before he could swim the few short strokes until he reached the small figure, who was splashing about with his arms above his head in the choppy, icy water.

Ethan grabbed both of Peter's wrists and dragged him upwards until he could take the boy's weight around his shoulders. He tried to calm the teenager, who was grabbing, scrabbling onto Ethan. Peter's sodden clothes and boots almost pulled them both headfirst into the waves, but Ethan was too quick and leant backwards, taking the full weight of the coughing, spluttering and panicking boy towards him.

In a few exhausting strokes, Ethan managed to drag their two bodies closer to the boat, where he could see that Mari was already at the side, waiting. Even so, it took precious few minutes to swim close enough so that he could support the thrashing boy around the waist and hoist Peter into his own boat and Mari's waiting arms, where he collapsed onto his side, coughing and heaving water, but alive and breathing.

Ethan waited until they were both safe and out

of the way before hauling himself, painfully and slowly, over the side and onto the deck, where he forced air into his lungs, before looking around for Mari. Hoping that she could get them back to shore on her own.

To his relief Mari had already moved over to the outboard motor and they were underway. The light from the cellphone pressed to her mouth illuminating her terrified pale face. Her coat was gone, wrapped around Peter, who was crying and shivering with shock and cold. Her hair was wet and hanging in strings around her face and her clothes were ruined.

And she had never looked more beautiful.

Ethan thought he heard her calling for help before the cold shakes hit him hard and he wrapped his arms tight across his chest. Cold. But with an icy fury burning inside of him.

Mari stood outside the emergency room where Peter was laughing about something with two younger-looking boys while his mother watched, her face tired and lined. She peeked through the slats in the window at the smiling teenager hooked up to the monitors, and the cluster of people around him.

Peter had given them all a terrible scare—her most of all.

Almost back to normal. That was how the nurse described her patient.

Well, that was not how she was feeling. *Far from it.*

She slumped against the wall, exhausted. And very angry with herself for being so weak and feeble that a simple accident had the power to destroy her completely.

It was all so confusing. She had turned against Ethan for surviving the accident that killed her brother, and yet she was so grateful that he had been there at that moment last night when she'd needed help, and he had not hesitated for one second to dive into the icy water to do what he could to rescue a boy he had only come to know a few days earlier.

Shaking, Mari staggered the few steps to the waiting area and collapsed, her head back, eyes closed, trying to catch her breath and persuade her heart to return to a normal beat. Adrenaline, fear and concern surged through her.

She was immediately taken back to the moments they had shared on the shore, and the tenderness of Ethan's touch. Ethan had recognised what she needed at that moment and offered it to her, before she knew it herself.

He truly had become a very special man.

She had trusted Ethan. Without thinking about it, or judging him, she had wanted to kiss him, back then, at the water's edge, and stay in the warmth of his embrace. She had wanted it very badly.

And why not?

They were adults. They were single. This wasn't the school holidays any more. All she had to do was put the past behind her and forget the pain that they both had suffered together and maybe they had a chance…

But what about the fact that she had three or four years of hard work ahead of her in renovating the house, working to earn the money she needed, and then, eventually, setting up and running her own IT business in Swanhaven? While Ethan's life was in Florida. Thousands of miles away.

Long-distance relationships were impossible.

A cold sense of reality washed over Mari. As cold as the air at the harbour.

Maybe, just maybe, there was a chance that they could spend more time together—but that was all it could be. And the sooner she realised that, the better for both of them. They could still care about one another as old friends, and she could treasure that friendship during the long months and years of lonely work she had ahead of her.

That was it. They could meet up now and then when he came to visit his parents at their retirement beach house and have a few drinks. No strings.

No strings?

And just who did she think she was kidding with that idea?

In the space of twenty-four hours she had

bought the home she had been dreaming about and working towards over the past years, was in debt to Ethan for loaning her the money and had then found out that her sister had no intention of staying in Swanhaven. Oh—and then she had to go out in a small boat to rescue a young sailor who seemed to idolise Ethan as much as she had. If that were possible.

All in all, not the quietest of Valentine weekends.

Mari sighed out loud, but turned it into a smile as the doctor strolled out of the cubicle where Ethan had been checked, leaving the curtain partially open, and from her waiting area Mari could see that the great hero was up and about, pulling on the collection of clothing that Rosa had brought in, courtesy of their extended family.

Of course Ethan had tried to make her feel better and had laughed away the threat of hypothermia and frostbite on the way here in the ambulance. Just testing the water before deciding it was a tad cold for a skinny dip—*but roll on the summer, eh?*

And all that came only a few hours after she had accused him of not knowing who she was. Stupid girl. He knew exactly who she was. Because he was her friend. Perhaps, if she tried hard enough, she might be able to see him in that way.

Time to face Ethan—and everything he had done for her. And see how looking at him as her new best friend worked.

Well, she could try! For both of their sakes.

She took a deep breath and strolled over to the door jamb and knocked once before peering around the curtain of the cubicle across the corridor.

'Nice pullover!' She grinned and folded her arms in as casual a pose as she could manage, considering that this was a hospital and the man she was looking at had been holding her not so very long ago.

Ethan pulled the pale blue and white-check V-neck sweater down over his hips, and then bent over to slip on the golfing shoes, complete with tassels.

'Only if you like the golfer look. And, believe

me, after living in Florida for so many years, this is my idea of style. Plus it's warm and dry and I think the shoes go particularly well.' He glanced up at her as he pushed himself off the bed.

'How are you doing, Mari? Warmed up a bit?'

She grinned at his roughly dried hair. 'More than a bit. How about you?'

'I'm good. All my fingers and toes are intact and apparently I have the constitution of a small ox. Have you talked to Peter?'

'Mild hypothermia from finding out just how cold the water can be, and swallowing quite a lot of it in the process, but he got a nasty shock—and so did his mother. They'll keep him here overnight, but he should be discharged in the morning.'

She paused and then glanced into his face.

'I can't remember if I thanked you last night. Isn't that terrible? You saved that boy's life and I might not have thanked you. You were amazing. Thank you, Ethan. He owes you. We all do.'

He was standing now, shrugging on a ski jacket several sizes too small which probably belonged to one of the cousins, but he looked up as though startled at her question, and stepped forward so that they were only inches apart. His voice was low and trembling with emotion when he spoke.

'I should be thanking you for staying with me, Mari. I know that it doesn't change the past. But thank you.'

The shock of those words, and the intensity with which they had been spoken, acted like a detonator under a firework.

Mari looked up into Ethan's face in amazement, her sore red eyes brimming with tears, and what she saw there broke her heart.

In that moment she recognised the compassion, and the good man that he had become. Had always been. He had gone into the freezing water to save a boy he barely knew who needed his help—but that was not what he meant at all. He was talking about Kit.

She had no words to express her feelings. Words would not be good enough.

Mari raised both hands open-palmed and pressed her fingertips against the sides of Ethan's face, as though she was holding a precious porcelain object, the stubble on his chin prickling against her wrists as her eyes locked on to his.

She moved her body forward so his back was tight against the sludge-green painted walls of the hospital room, pressed her chest against his, closed her eyes and in one smooth movement tilted her head just enough so that when she kissed him their bodies were a perfect fit.

This was what she'd wanted on the shore.

This was what she had been denying herself with pathetic attempts to pretend that Ethan was nothing more than an old childhood friend, every doubt and hesitancy had been blown away by a few simple words which expanded her world into areas where rational thoughts about where this could take them in the future did not matter any more.

The thrill of his warm mouth on hers quivered through her body, warming, relaxing, exploring. Her heart thumped and her breathing became hot and ragged as she moved into his embrace, her entire body revelling in the wonder of the experience.

Ethan's head moved sideways to lock with hers as she took a breath, and his hand pressed the back of her head towards him for a second deeper kiss.

His other hand was around her back now, drawing her closer, and the pressure of his fingers seemed to lift her higher and higher, her heart racing as Ethan returned the kiss, his mouth harder, wider and hotter.

He was kissing her back with a passion and intensity she had only dreamt about as a girl and in those lonely dreams through all of the years since.

It was everything she could have imagined, and every nerve in her body sang with the thrill of the feel of his warm mouth on hers.

The first time they'd kissed they'd been teenagers, and this was a world away. This was a powerful, handsome athlete of a man who held her in his arms with such delight and passion it was ridiculous to resist. And she didn't want to.

It was Ethan who broke the kiss, the palms of his hands sliding down to her waistline. His head moved forward as she lifted away, and she was stunned to see that his eyes were still closed, his mouth open, as he tried to keep contact as long as possible.

His lips pressed into her forehead as his arms circled her waist, as though determined to keep the physcial bond between them as long as possible, so that his lips could move from her hair to her brow in one smooth motion.

She felt she could stay there for ever. Locked in his embrace.

He was her rock, the support she had been looking for all of her life.

This was the Ethan she had dreamt of.

His hands moved from her waist to her head and gently drew her back, away from him so that he could look into her face.

Her straggly hair. Her red eyes.

'Perhaps I should learn to swim after all?' She smiled. 'Just in case you're not here to rescue me.'

He said nothing. He stroked her hair back

behind her ears as his eyes scanned her face, his thumbs brushing her cheeks, and he just breathed, breathed and looked into her face as though it was the most fascinating thing he had ever seen.

As though looking for something.

Whatever it was, he found it.

Ethan pressed both hands tight around her face and hair, took half a step forward, their eyes still locked. And he drew a deep breath.

As though by magic and some unspoken signal, Mari's mouth opened just in time as Ethan kissed her harder than any other man had ever kissed her, the passion of the connection so intense, so forceful, Mari automatically flung her arms around his neck to stop herself from falling backwards, the power of this man's body concentrated, focused into one single connection between two mouths.

She couldn't breathe, couldn't think of anything except kissing him back, pressure for pressure, movement for movement, her hot panting breath fighting to keep up with his.

He moved position, sliding his mouth across her lips, lifting her face with his thumbs and locking it to his.

Something in the back of her brain registered that there was movement and female voices in the corridor and, as the curtain twitched, Ethan broke the kiss. And she opened her eyes.

His eyes were wild, carnivorous. Full of passion and love. And questions.

Neither of them said anything but just stood there, her arms still wrapped around his neck, his hands now pressed into her back, then slowly, slowly, he started to breathe and the fire in his eyes calmed as he drew her closer, pressing her head into his shoulder, one of his hands moving up and down her back, the other still at her waist.

Mari closed her eyes for a second, revelling in the heat of the sensation, listening to their breathing, feeling his heart still thumping hard under his chest.

And she knew. If they had been alone in this room she would not have stopped kissing him.

She wanted to feel his touch on her skin. She

wanted him to show her how much he cared about her in the most intimate way.

And if this was any indication of the passion this man could feel, he wanted the same. He wanted her just as much as she wanted him.

Which meant only one thing.

She was in serious trouble.

CHAPTER NINE

MARI spread the bundles of photographs out across the sofa and tried to make some sense of the collection. It had been her father's idea to give Mari a grown-up camera for her twelfth birthday, and it had immediately become one of her trademarks. Whenever she left the house, the stiff brown leather camera case came with her, stuffed into pockets, satchels and school bags with a spare roll of film, just in case.

In fact people used to joke that Mari was always the one at the back of the room taking the photographs of other people enjoying themselves while she looked on. She never thought that funny or odd, just a fact of life that was all part and parcel of being the academic one. The quiet one. Not a bit like her brother or younger sister.

She hadn't minded really. It gave her a reason

to be there and not have to talk. And here were the prints to prove it. Her parents, her extended family, so many Christmases and birthdays—it was all there, including some lovely ones of her mother which she set aside to scan for her own album.

Mari quickly sorted through the last bundle, selecting group shots of Ethan and his parents at a prize-giving, a summer party, and what looked like the end of the Regatta dance.

Her fingers lingered over two photos of Kit and Ethan from some junior yacht club event. Gangly, awkward limbs and wide smiles. But it was their energy and passion for life which beamed out at her from the photograph. They were both so young and happy and bursting with enthusiasm with a brilliant future ahead of them.

Ethan had come a long way and had realised his dreams. While Kit had had his snatched away from him in an instant. Just like Peter almost had.

Mari closed her eyes for a second and pressed the photograph against her chest. Ethan had saved Peter's life last night and the horror of that moment when she had seen Peter in the water was captured forever in her mind; had been there every time she had drifted in and out of sleep.

It shouldn't matter that Peter was shy and quiet, and that she saw a little of herself in him too, but it did. He had been brave enough to take a boat out on the water alone—but there was no way that he could have seen the heavy tree trunk which was lying almost submerged, just under the waterline. Until it was too late.

Her eyes pricked with tears. She had tried *not* to compare Peter's accident with what had happened to Kit, but it was impossible. She had been there last night and had seen how confused and disorientated Peter had been. Alone and in shock, he'd been too bewildered to help himself in those few crucial minutes in the icy water and his heavy clothes had dragged him down.

And just for a second she had an insight into how Ethan must have felt that day at the regatta when the wave had hit their boat. Only last night Ethan had dived into the water to try and save Peter, instead of being thrown into the water.

Ethan the man had taken control, while Ethan the boy would have been just as confused and shocked as Peter had been.

Why had she not seen that before? Ethan was blaming himself for an accident that had not been his fault. And that was just wrong.

Just as she had been wrong about a lot of things.

Wiping away a tear from the corner of her eye, Mari put down her photo albums and settled on the couch with her feet tucked under her, the unheated room quite chilly now the light was fading.

The past few days had been unsettling; her mind felt giddy and out of control. As though she was spinning round and round on a carousel, unable to get off even though it was making her feel dizzy and shaking and unable to hold back her feelings and emotions.

And right at the centre of that carousel was Ethan. Somehow he was able to strip away all of the carefully constructed barriers which she had created around her heart. He had always had that power and the intensity of how she felt about him scared her. And thrilled her beyond measure.

She exhaled slowly. Tasks. Work. That was the answer. She had to focus on working through these photographs as a leaving present.

Leaving? Last night at the hospital had felt like the start of something. Not the end.

Mari sat up straighter on the sofa and blinked to clear her head.

She had just opened the first album when there was a knock on the kitchen door and a loud, 'Hello,' in a man's voice—Ethan's voice.

'In here,' she called out, trying to sound casual and failing miserably, probably due to the thumping of her heart and the lump in her throat.

He stuck his head around the door and smiled.

The sight of his face hit her in the bottom of her gut like a punch, leaving her breathless and dizzy. The blood rushed to her head. Hot. Thumping. Her heart racing with delight at seeing him again.

'You left your laptop bag in my boat yesterday!'

She had to laugh at that. Just when she'd thought he might be here to offer his undying love and beg her to run away with him to the sunshine, and all Ethan wanted was to return her bag—the bag she usually carried everywhere with her, but somehow she had totally forgotten about it in the rush to get Peter and Ethan ashore.

'Yes, I suppose I did. Can you leave it in the hall? Thank you.'

'No problem.' He looked at the albums on the sofa. 'What have you got there?'

Mari took the plunge and gestured him over with one hand.

As he collapsed down onto the sofa next to her and stretched out his long denim-clad legs, she passed him the first volume.

To her delight, he extended one of his arms along the back of the sofa and she felt instantly warmer and somehow safer inside that embrace.

'I've decided that you need some personal photos in that splendid house of yours from your wicked and evil past. I'm sure your parents would love to have a record of Swanhaven through the ages,' she lied confidently. 'So, if you've got a minute, I could use the help.'

'Now why didn't I think about that? Of course I need personal photographs. Great idea.' Ethan started flicking through the pages before yelling out a, 'Wow!'

Mari practically leapt back in recoil. 'What?'

She leant sideways to look at the page Ethan was holding out as though it was toxic.

'Well, just look at that,' Mari whispered, not daring to look at Ethan in case she burst out laughing. 'Mr Chandler at his first Regatta dance. How old were you then? Fourteen?'

'Fourteen and a half and, boy, I had forgotten those hipster trousers! Maybe I thought sparkly was cool back then.' He pretended to shiver in horror.

'What about the matching skirts Mum made for Rosa and me? She was going through a phase of dressing us both up in identical outfits back then. Rosa hated it.'

Ethan chuckled. 'I remember. It caused chaos. Same clothes, same hair, same bag. It was like having double vision until you opened your mouth.'

His fingers played with the back of her hair, lifting strands above the collar of the hand-knit sweater she had borrowed from Rosa. 'I love what you've done with your hair. Elegant and stylish. It suits you.'

Mari felt her neck flush scarlet and pressed her lips together to stifle a giggle. 'Thank you.' Then she quickly changed the subject by pointing to a group photo. 'The high school science fair.' Mari shook her head. 'I had forgotten about that.'

'Your model was the San Andreas Fault system. Complete with a working friction model of the fault and photo displays.'

Mari turned around and stared, only too aware that her mouth had dropped slightly open in shock as Ethan continued, 'You had tectonic plates and ocean fissures, and could have been filmed for a TV documentary.'

'I can't believe that you remembered that,' Mari whispered, shaking her head. 'That has to be twelve years ago. It was the very last week at school before the summer holiday and Kit was so annoyed when you turned up with your parents while we were still trapped in the classroom.'

'I recall everything about that science fair. It changed my life.'

'What do you mean? Changed your life? You developed a passion for geological faults which made you turn to a life on the ocean wave?' Mari replied with a suppressed chuckle, suddenly concerned that this blast from the past was taking her to places she did not want to go after all. And it had nothing to do with models of geological fault systems.

Only Ethan didn't laugh, but focused on the photo in his hand.

'I looked at that model and the photo display, and then I looked around and saw you, just sitting at the back of the classroom with your head in a book. Oblivious to everyone else. All alone. Contained. And that's when I knew.'

He looked up at her and their eyes locked.

'Every other person in the class had done the minimum amount of work they'd needed to create a model to get the praise. The marks, the points, whatever. Not you. You didn't need me or Kit or Rosa or anyone else to validate you as a person. You spent the time making it perfect because that was who you were and the standards you set for yourself were so high—and so demanding that no boy was ever going to come up to those standards. I just wasn't good enough for you. Intellectually or as a person. It was a blow.'

Mari looked into his face and saw the kind of pain she had never seen before. No joking. This was real. 'I don't understand. All I can remember is that you teased me for days about how long I had spent working on it indoors, while I could have been outside at the beach with the rest of the family You were always making cutting remarks about me having my head in a book.'

'Don't you see? That was why I teased you. I was so attracted to you but I knew that you were so far out of my league that it was a joke. You weren't responsible for my massive inferiority complex. I was.'

'You liked me? I mean, you really liked me? I had no clue.'

Ethan chuckled and found something fascinating to look at in the hollow below Mari's ear. 'I made sure that you didn't. In fact, if it hadn't been for the big fight we had at your birthday, I probably would never had summoned up the courage to even try and kiss you. Until that moment I thought that you hated me. You'd closed down on me, and I didn't know how to reach you.'

Mari blew out. *Hard.*

'I didn't hate you, Ethan. I hated what Kit's death had done to my life and my family. They were destroyed. Nothing was ever going to be the same again. And when my dad didn't turn up on my birthday after I had waited all day? I was clever enough to know that the happy life I had known was finished. Over. For good.'

Mari swallowed down hard and blinked away tears before she gave Ethan a half smile. 'You came out to the beach and then followed me to the house. You were a convenient target. And I am so sorry for all of the horrible things that I said to you. I was so unfair. Can you forgive me?'

Ethan reached forward and gathered Mari into

his arms, his chin pressed onto the top of her hair, and she sucked in deep breaths against his chest.

'There's nothing to forgive. I blamed myself for wanting to be with you and hold you even though I felt responsible for breaking up your wonderful family. I felt guilty that I kissed you and didn't know what to do about it the next day, so I left. Even though I knew in my heart that you would probably hate me for it.'

'Why? Why did you want me to hate you?'

Mari lifted her head so that she could look into Ethan's eyes.

'Oh, that's easy. I felt that I didn't deserve anything better. To see you cry, to hear your pain and suffering…that was so hard. I couldn't deal with it. I didn't know how.'

'Oh, Ethan. We were both grieving, I can see that, but why are you telling me this now?'

He shrugged. 'I thought you ought to know that I have never been more grateful that Kit chose me to be his friend and I had the privilege of knowing you and your family. That's all.'

She looked at him and then broke into a smile.

'You were a good team. No doubt about that. Kit loved the time he spent with you on the water.'

'We were the best. Nobody got close. Ethan Chandler and Kit Chance. How many times was that read out at the award ceremonies?'

'Damn right.'

Mari glanced up at him and realised that his eyes had never left her face. He wasn't looking at the photographs any more. *Just her.*

'I was looking for photos of Kit. We haven't really talked about him, have we?'

Her throat was suddenly dry and tight.

Ethan tilted his head. 'There's no need to. He's there in every conversation we ever had. Your family blamed me for his death, and I understand that completely and would probably feel the same in your shoes. I was in the boat, and I should have been able to save him. And I couldn't. There's not a week goes by, even now, when I don't see someone who reminds me of Kit. That never goes away.'

'No. It doesn't. We know that you tried to save him that day. But we're not fools. We all knew that Kit was so headstrong and so determined to beat you. He took too many risks and my dad… my dad let him do it. He was the parent and he was in the boat that day when you misjudged the wave and it caught the boat. And Kit…'

Ethan's reply was a long intake of breath, followed by a sharp nod.

'Kit went over and hit his head on the side of your dad's boat when it came alongside. And it killed him. You can say it, Mari. We both lost a wonderful friend that day. And your dad lost his son. And I'm sorry. I'm sorry that he died. More than I can say. Seeing you again also brought it home to me that I've not been very fair with my own parents. Kit was having fun that day, while I chose to put myself into the most dangerous waters on the planet. And that's not fair on them, or on anyone who cares about me. It's a hard life when you turn your back on those you love.'

Mari closed the covers of the photo album and pressed her fingers hard against the cover. 'You're right. You are selfish. But you know what you want and you go for it. And I respect that.

But everything has changed, Ethan. You, Rosa and especially me. I'm not the sweet little daddy's girl I was back then. And Kit has gone and won't be coming back. I suppose there has to be a time when we decide to move forward, or stay trapped in the past.'

Her voice let her down, the burning tears she had held back pricking the back of her eyes.

'Then come to the Valentine dance with me tonight. As my date.'

Mari's head shot up and she blinked away tears of astonishment. 'You're asking me out on a date? You? Ethan Chandler, yachtsman extraordinaire?'

'How about Ethan, an old family friend? Does that make it easier to say yes? Because I would really like it if you did say yes. Please. Take a risk, Mari. Take a risk on enjoying yourself. What do you say? I thought that I didn't deserve a chance of happiness when Kit had his chances taken away from him. Maybe I was wrong about that. And I would like to find out more.'

And, without waiting for her answer, his hands came up to cup her chin and he pressed his full warm lips onto hers in a kiss so tender that she wanted it to go on for ever.

Her eyes were still closed when he slid his hands away. 'I'll pick you up at eight.' Then he gave her nose a gentle tap and, without waiting for her reply, he walked out of the door, leaving Mari sitting in silence, her heart thumping and a wide grin on her face. Only then did she dare to breathe.

It was two minutes before eight and Mari had been peeking out of the window every few minutes for the last half hour since Rosa left. *Just in case.*

So why was it that she was fluffing the sofa cushions to try and calm her nerves when she heard the gentle knock at the door? So that she practically stumbled in her haste to open it?

Ethan was wearing the smartest, sexiest dinner suit that she had ever seen.

He had shaved. His hair was swept back and styled. He was wearing shiny black shoes and a shirt so white she might need sunglasses if the fluorescent lights were working at the club.

All he needed now was a pair of sunglasses and he'd pass for a Hollywood movie star.

Ethan Chandler looked stunning, and her poor sensitive heart did a little flip. This was *her* date for the evening. *Oh, yes. Was that possible?*

Gulping away a sense that she was totally out of her depth here, Mari nodded slowly as she tried desperately to come up with a witty comment which would not betray her total wistful joy at seeing this man standing on her sister's doorstep.

'Um…I can see that your life as a fashion model was not entirely wasted. Looking good, Ethan.'

'Oh, this little old thing?' he joked and brushed an imaginary speck of dust from his jacket and then gave a low snort and his face instantly relaxed. 'I took myself off to Swanchester this afternoon and threw myself at the mercy of a menswear shop who specialise in formal wear. It was a new experience. But I like challenges. And these are for you.'

Ethan regally lifted up a small but perfect bouquet of the most beautiful roses, freesias and tropical greenery and made a small bow before presenting her with the flowers.

'I have no idea what kind of flowers you like, but my mum loves these. Are they okay?' he asked through gritted teeth.

Mari took the bouquet with both of her hands and brought the flowers to her nose so that she could drink in the heavenly scent. 'Oh, that is so gorgeous. I adore freesias. It's like summer in one place. Yes, they are okay. In fact they are better than okay. Thank you.'

Ethan blew out one long breath of relief, then thrust his chin out and wriggled a forefinger down under his stiff white shirt collar.

'Comfy? Mari asked, chewing the inside of her cheek to fight down her laughter.

Ethan lifted his head and regally raked the fingers of his right hand back through his hair. Then relaxed and grinned at her.

'Not in the least. But my suffering is all in a good cause. This is our first date. I think it's traditional for the boy to be dressed by his mother for this rite of passage. I had to improvise.'

Mari stepped forward to straighten Ethan's black bow tie, making sure that, as she did so, their bodies were in contact from hips to chest. Her reward was the telltale increase in his breathing so that she could almost hear the beat of his heart under her hands.

'You look fine. Just. Fine.'

She dared to glance up and blushed from neck to toe at the look she saw in Ethan's eyes, which was positively indecent.

Sliding back down from tiptoe to the floor along the length of his body was no hardship at all.

'Every Valentine Fairy should have her prince. And I think you will do quite nicely.'

Mari caressed the front of Ethan's shirt, sensing the bands of muscle that lay beneath the fine fabrics. Gulping down something close to exuberance, she gave his chest one final pat, then stepped back.

'Don't I have the chance to see your dress for

the evening?' he replied. 'Although your shoes are quite delightful.'

Mari looked down at her snow boots, which were sticking out from below her long padded winter coat, and waggled her toes.

'Ah. There's a reason for that. Think of it as a surprise. There's been a slight change of plan.' Mari sucked in a breath. 'Rosa had agreed to be the Valentine Fairy for the kids tonight at the party. Only with her arm out of action, she asked me to take her place.'

She pushed her lips together. 'I am so sorry about this, but the Valentine Fairy is quite a tradition in Swanhaven and I couldn't let the children down. The good news is that I only have to work for my supper for about half an hour, and then the rest of the evening is ours. Is that okay? Because Rosa has already gone ahead with all the props we need. And she says thank you for your understanding.'

Ethan smoothed back a wisp of hair which had fallen forward onto Mari's brow.

'Well, this is going to be a first in more ways

than one. I've never had the pleasure of a date with a Valentine Fairy. It almost makes me feel special. Even if it does mean sharing my date with the good citizens of the town.'

'Then I shall have to make it up to you, won't I?' Mari said, fluttering her eyelashes at him. 'And the sooner we get the party started, the sooner we can really start our date.'

'I like the sound of that even more. Shall we go, my lady? Your carriage awaits.'

'One more minute.' Suddenly inspired, Mari reached into the bouquet of roses and freesias and selected a full pink rose and presented it to Ethan.

'Would you do the honours of completing my fairy crown, kind prince?'

'I would be honoured,' Ethan replied and pressed the stem of the rose into her hair behind her right ear, his fingers lingering on her cheek as he secured the blossom. Then they moved in slow circles across her temple into the wave of curls which had taken Rosa an hour to spray tight, and down into her neck.

'That's perfect. You are perfect.'

She could not resist it. She giggled. A proper girly giggle. Then stretched out both of her hands and gently clasped hold of Ethan's.

'Now look what you've done.' She laughed. 'Our first date and I am giggling already.'

And they just stood there, holding hands, smiling at one another like teenagers, as though nothing else mattered in the world.

It had taken Ethan five minutes to park his car in the snow, after dropping Mari at the entrance to the yacht club, and he opened the door just as a great round of cheering and applause went up from the other partygoers. He strode inside to see what all the excitement was about.

And instantly stopped in his tracks, scarcely believing what he was seeing.

Rosa and Mari Chance were skipping, arm in arm, into the clubhouse. But it was their choice of party-wear that was the main cause of the excitement.

Rosa and Mari were wearing identical pink

ballet tutus and tight sparkly tops, waving tinsel wands with glitter stars at the ends. Plastic tiaras completed the ensemble, tied under the chin with a pink ribbon tied in a huge flower bow. Mari's crown was decorated with the pink rose and, apart from the strapping on Rosa's arm, they could have been twins.

And they were laughing like loons. Real laughter. The kind of laughter only sisters and close family could create in rare moments. He had missed that.

The magic fairy wands did not go unnoticed by the older members of the Chance extended family, who simply shook their heads and mumbled something about the crazy sisters and the dangers of alcohol at this time of year.

He thought they looked fabulous.

As for those legs? Those long, long legs? Well, it seemed that some things had improved over the years. Mari was about two inches taller than Rosa and he could look at her legs all night. She was wearing tiny ballet shoes with pink ribbons winding up each calf. Oh, boy.

At least they were a distraction from the tight tops. And he was not the only one to notice. Half the young and not-so-young single men in the room had abandoned their Valentine dates and made a beeline for the girls, who were obliging with twirls of their ballet skirts.

This was too good to miss, so Ethan resisted the temptation to reclaim his date and decided to watch for once and allow someone else to be the centre of attention.

The local police officer won a round of applause for pretending to arrest Rosa for causing a public disturbance, only Rosa stole his police hat while he was concentrating on writing down the details of the pink garter she was wearing, and he had to chase after her out of the door and onto the harbour, leaving Mari laughing her head off, calling out, 'Officer in hot pursuit.'

Where had this Mari come from?

He stared for a moment and listened to her laughter. Laughter so genuine and real that it eased its way into his heart like a great fire and stayed there, warming him through and through.

She really was quite remarkable.

And then she was swallowed up by the rest of her family, just as the Chairman of the Yacht Club came up to shake Ethan's hand. Did he have a few minutes to talk to him and Mrs Morris about how they would keep up Peter's sailing lessons? Apparently last night's accident had made Peter even keener to carry on. Ethan looked over one shoulder just in time to see Mari settling down with a cluster of exuberant, energetic ladies and decided that he could spare a couple of minutes. Just a couple.

By the time Ethan returned from supplying the entire yacht club with enough mulled wine to intoxicate a small army, he had somehow agreed to find Peter a place on one of his training ships and Mari was sitting on a bar chair, surrounded by a group of young girls listening intently to the story she was telling. She lowered the book just long enough to stare intently into the faces of each child in turn as she begged them to believe in fairies, who could give every girl and boy Valentine wishes and kisses.

A great chorus called out, 'We believe. We believe.'

Ah. Peter Pan and Tinkerbell. Nice one. The book snapped closed, the mothers clapped in applause and drifted away to eat burgers and hot dogs and chicken legs, each child taking a tiny tinsel star from Mari as they came for their hug.

Ethan casually strolled up and picked up a fallen star. 'Any hugs left, Tink?'

She looked up from refastening her thin-soled ballet shoes, seemingly unaware that she was displaying a healthy amount of leg in the process.

'You have to be under ten and female to qualify. And preferably less than six feet tall.'

'Ah! My faith has been restored. Ageist, sexist and heightist! All qualities to admire in the average Valentine's Day Fairy. Speaking of which—I thought *Peter Pan* was a Christmas story. You could be in great danger of confusing a lot of people here tonight.'

He casually returned her tinsel wand. 'Not that I'm complaining,' he added with a wink. 'Especially in that outfit! It truly is quite remarkable and I am officially a lucky man.'

Mari looked down at her pale pink pumps and wiggled her toes inside her pink tights. 'You can consider this a special performance. One night only. Never to be repeated.'

'Shame. So far, it is totally working. Where did Rosa find those costumes?'

'Apparently there are boxes of clothes up in her attic. My loving sister gave me two choices. It was either the Christmas Wish fairy or Mum's Dorothy costume. Complete with ruby slippers and a stuffed toy Toto that barks if you pull a string.'

Ethan nodded. 'No contest. I particularly like the tiara. It pulls the whole thing together.'

Mari reached up and touched the plastic rings with the crystal lampshade droplets.

'I think it suits me. Rosa looks weird. But on me? Cute. It's the rose that makes all the difference.'

She peeked out at him between her eyelashes

and tried out a wide-eyed cheeky grin before asking, 'Do you think I look cute, Ethan?'

'You look very special, Miss Chance. Cute does not cover it.'

Mari curtseyed, holding out one side of her tutu, and then paused and waved her wand as a family passed by, then looked at him, hard, before going on, her eyes never leaving his face. 'There is another reason my lovely sister per-suaded me to come dressed like this and make a fool of myself.' Mari sucked in a breath and the words gushed out. 'Now that Rosa is leaving Swanhaven to run a craft shop, this could be our last opportunity to be here as sisters. It's the end of an era, Ethan.'

Ethan looked out across the crowd and ges-tured towards Rosa as she chatted to friends and neighbours. 'Then good luck to her. That's a brave decision. Who knows? Maybe there will be two Chance sister entrepreneurs out in the world soon. That's a very scary thought.'

He gestured across to the barbecue with one thumb. 'So. Want a hot dog, Tink? Barbecue?

You're going to need sustenance before I take you dancing!'

Mari shook her head in disbelief. 'The mulled wine is starting to kick in on an empty stomach. Because I thought you just asked me to dance. And you don't dance!'

Ethan smiled and planted his hands on his hips before nodding. 'Nothing gets past you, girl. I thought it was time to make an effort. Show you a few new moves I've picked up over the years.'

He reached out and meshed his fingers into hers. 'Come on. Take a risk, Mari. This could be your last chance.'

Mari sighed as Ethan stepped back, drawing her from the plastic chair, and was fluffing out her tutu one-handed to brave dancing in public with the most handsome man in the room when Rosa almost ran up to them.

'Come on, you two. The line dancing is just about to start and I've saved you a place in the front row. What are you waiting for? Get this show on the road. Let's rock this joint.'

Mari looked at Ethan. Ethan looked at Mari,

then he stood ramrod straight, reached out, seized Mari's hand and whispered the magical words, 'I'll risk it if you will.'

CHAPTER TEN

'THIS has been quite some day!' Mari managed a faint smile as Ethan opened the passenger door of his car, and then shivered when the freezing-cold air hit her.

Without asking, Ethan slid off his sheepskin coat and wrapped it around her shoulders, before sliding one arm under her legs. 'Here. This coat suits you better than me. Keep it. And you'll never make it across the sludge in those magical slippers, Tinkerbell.'

Mari's arms instinctively wrapped around Ethan's neck as he swung her out of the seat, pushed the car door closed with his foot and strolled calmly down the path to Rosa's doorstep as though she weighed nothing and this was something he did every day of the week.

He didn't speak and she couldn't form the words. Her personal space expanded to include

Ethan and it felt so amazing, so precious, that somehow words would only ruin the moment.

The movement of his steps ended only too soon, and he stood in the light of the porch. He simply looked down at her and her heart melted.

His arm moved slightly so that her legs slid gently to the sparkling frost of the stone step.

'Thank you,' she murmured. 'For the coat. For last night. And for being there today. I don't know if I could have got through it without you. And, most of all, thank you for tonight. I had a great time.'

Ethan's other arm freed itself from around her waist to press against her back as he opened his mouth to speak, then shook his head and lowered it so that his brow was pressed against her forehead. His breathing was hard and fast against her cheek as he opened his mouth to say something, then changed his mind and braved a small smile.

Whatever he wanted to say was probably not going to be good, but she knew she had to hear it before she changed her mind.

* * *

'Look at me,' she whispered. 'You can tell me. I may not like it, but after the day I've just had, I don't think anything could surprise me.'

Mari reached out and meshed her fingers with Ethan's as her eyes scanned his face. The blue of his eyes was iridescent in the reflection from the snow, from the streetlights and the warm glow from Rosa's cottage. His tan was a distant memory. His cheeks were burning red, and his lips were tinged with cold.

He looked absolutely gorgeous.

'Perhaps that gives me some hope that maybe, just maybe, you might let me into your life one of these fine days. And forgive me for surviving that accident when Kit died, because I'm not sure I can do it on my own.'

'Ethan!' She had started to speak, desperate to tell him that he was the last person who needed to be forgiven and the past was the past, but he gently pressed one fingertip to her lips.

'Please let me finish. I need to say this now. Or not say it at all.'

She dropped her hand, but meshed her fingers

even tighter into Ethan's, feeling him give reassuring pressure back.

'Let me introduce myself. I am Ethan
Francis Chandler. The international yachtsman
and, more recently, a new up-and-coming sailing
instructor and charity worker. My name has been
mentioned in magazines and on TV. My parents
even have press cuttings, can you believe that?
I can sail just about anything you throw at me
from a raft to a super-yacht. I can cook. I can iron
my own shirts. I have friends who actually like
to go out with me to eat and drink. And enjoy
themselves! In my company! And you…you are
the most angry, most competitive, most challenging, most guarded and most stubborn woman I
have ever met. What the hell is so wrong with
you that you won't accept that I could care about
you? And let yourself care about me right back?'

His voice was trembling now, the gaze in his
eyes intense.

'I left Swanhaven to get away from you, and
everything you made me feel, Mari Chance.
The guilt about Kit and the pain of leaving your

family like that has stayed with me every day of these last years. And seeing you here? Like this? Suddenly I'm seventeen again and just as confused and totally mesmerised by you as I was then. But some things are clear. I've been a fool, Mari. Ever since I met you at the jetty I knew that this was a second chance for us to finish what we started. We could make a future together. And that comes before anything else.'

Ethan broke eye contact to look around the snow-covered narrow streets that led down to the harbour and then back to Mari, who was staring intensely at his face, focusing on every word, every syllable coming out of his lips.

His breath was hot, fast. 'I have a wonderful job sharing my passion with kids like Peter. I have a lovely house and a great future ahead of me. And yet I still have that burning passion to sail away to some distant ocean to get away from my pain and my loss. After last night, and what has happened between us these past few days, I'm starting to realise that maybe, just maybe, I could stop running away and trying to live the life Kit never had. But I can't do that on my own.'

The pressure of his fingers increased until it was almost painful.

'But I don't want to live a life without you in it, Mari. Because I need you and I want to know if you feel the same way…' He could not speak any more.

His hand came up and cupped her chin, his thumb moving into her hair as his head tilted. Cold lips pressed into her cheek, the cold burning against the hot sweaty tears as she closed her eyes to revel in the sensation. Their fingers disengaged as Ethan's hand wound around her waist and drew her closer to his body.

His lips moved across one eyelid, gently, gently, then down to her upper lip. The pressure increased only for a second as she swallowed down a shivering breath.

His kiss was everything she had imagined it would be.

Warm and loving, so very loving.

The smell of his skin.

Douglas Library
Tel: 00353 214924932

Borrowed Items 09/08/2019 10:18
XXXXXXXXXX1383

Item Title	Due Date
* The boy is back in town / Nina Harrington.	30/08/2019
His mistress with two secrets / Dani Collins.	23/08/2019
The sheikh's last seduction / Jennie Lucas.	23/08/2019

* Indicates items borrowed today

Thank you for using this unit

www.corkcitylibraries.ie/douglas
email support-uk@bibliotheca.com

The sensation of his stubble on her face.

The thumping of his heart. Racing now as he drew her closer and moved his hand further into her hair.

'Come and live with me in Florida. I could help you rebuild your house here in Swanhaven and we could come back any time you like—but this has to be your choice. Your decision.'

His forehead pressed against hers, the hot breath steaming as they both panted open-mouthed in the freezing night air. Alive in the moment. 'You can work there. Make a career for yourself. Your company even has an office in my city.'

He leant back just enough so that she could focus on his smile.

'I believe in you. And I believe in your talent. You can do anything you want to in this world. You don't need to wait to create your own business. You can start it in Florida and I will be right there, helping you every step of the way.'

His thumb was moving across her chin as he stared into her face.

'I know you can find a way to make it happen.

If you want it badly enough. So what do you say? Will you take the risk? Will you come back to Florida with me? We can do this if we work together.'

It was that final statement which broke the spell he had cast.

Mari inhaled the biting air and stepped back, desperate to regain some distance from this crazy intensity. She had not felt so scared for a long time.

'Oh, Ethan, I'm so confused. I was actually starting to think about how it would work, but this is too much for me to take in… I never imagined that…'

She looked into his shocked face and knew that it was going to hurt, no matter how much she wanted to prevent his pain.

'You know more than anyone how hard it was for me when my dad left, and then you left with your family. And it broke my heart. It's taken me ten years to build up the barriers I need to protect myself from that kind of pain and loss. My life is finally coming together and I don't know if I'm ready to take that kind of risk.'

'What kind of life do you truly have, Mari? Because I know exactly how lonely my existence has become in sunny Florida. What does a great job and a sea view matter without the things that are important? It isn't enough. Not nearly enough.'

He stroked her cheek and smiled gently, sensing that he had just exposed a nerve.

'I want to make my home with the girl I'm still crazy about. Come on. You don't need to live in your old home on your own. I could help you make it a home again. A real home with a future.'

She closed her eyes and steadied herself before looking into Ethan's face. 'I'm scared.'

Shaking her head in disbelief at her own words, Mari pushed away from Ethan and started pacing, her hands pushed deep into the coat pockets to thaw out.

'Maybe the timing is all wrong, but suddenly I feel that my life is in total turmoil. I'm not sure about anything any more.'

Before she could speak another syllable, Ethan stepped forward, grabbed her around the waist with two strong hands and drew her towards him, chest to chest. So close she could smell the tang of his sweat on his shirt, the faint trace of his aftershave. The Ethan smell. The Ethan presence, which filled the moment to bursting.

'Chandler and Chance,' he whispered in a voice designed to send heat to the frozen tips of her ballet shoes. 'If we could work together we would be unstoppable. But you're right, this has been a long day. Will you think about what I've said? Please. Think about it.'

He held her face between his cupped hands as she nodded, then glanced down and smiled. 'Your poor feet. Crazy girl. Goodnight, Mari. I'll drop by to see you in the morning. Sleep well.'

He kissed her forehead once. Barely more than a brush of his lips across her skin. It felt like a branding iron, burning a mark that would never be erased. Then he turned around and walked slowly down the path to his four-wheel drive, one hand thrust into each pocket of his jeans, leaving her standing, stunned, shivering even inside the coat still around her shoulders, just watching him start up the car and drive away.

He didn't look back.

And she just stood there.

She had to.

Her moist ballet shoes had frozen to the ice on the doorstep.

The wind had picked up during the night and it buffeted Mari as she made her way along the top of the cliff path heading away from the centre of Swanhaven and out towards the headland. And the house where she used to live. The house which was going to become her new home.

She'd been so confident that this time she had a real chance of reconnecting with her old life when she had been so happy, safe and warm in a family who loved her and valued her. A family she could trust to do the right thing for her and never once complain that she was distant or that she had let them down by being 'emotionally unavailable,' as her old boyfriend has described her. Inside the warm embrace of her family, she had never felt the need to close down her heart.

It was daylight now but still too early in the morning for anyone else to be on the path. She could see a few dog-walkers playing with their dogs on the beach below and she envied them their carefree moments of fun and laughter. But right now she was grateful for the solitude and the familiar soundtrack of the sea crashing onto the rocks at the point, the call of seabirds and the sound of the wind in the trees on the other side of the fields and the crunch of her own footsteps on the cold stone chippings and frosty grass as she walked.

It had been a long night which she had got through in snatches of broken sleep and much tossing and turning before finally giving up and heading downstairs to the empty, cold kitchen and a hot drink before facing all that her first day as a homeowner in Swanhaven could bring.

Starting with seeing Ethan again.

His face and his soft voice had echoed through her dreams, filling her with a sense of belonging and warmth and familiar contentment which was so at odds with the turmoil seething though her that she had seized on to it like a life raft in those dark and lonely moments when everything that had happened over the week threatened to overwhelm her.

And that was so wrong. And unfair. *To both of them.*

Last night he had offered her his heart and she had been too terrified to accept it.

When had she lost the ability to trust and show her emotions? Was it when Kit died and their father left them? Or when she lashed out at Ethan on her sixteenth birthday? She had only dared to kiss him when the strength of her pent-up frustrations and anguish and grief had overcome the barriers she had created to protect herself.

Reliving their tender moments together when they kissed in the hospital, it had been her overwhelming sense of relief that he and Peter were safe and well that had broken down the flimsy barricades and allowed her the luxury of being able to show Ethan how she truly felt about him.

More than that, the power of those feelings had given her the freedom to believe that she could be attractive and worthy of being loved by a man like Ethan. If only for a few moments, she had enjoyed that remarkable sensation that she was ready to trust in another person and fall in love with him. And she was worthy of that love.

Spending these past few days with Ethan had made her feel things that she had never felt before. Oh, she had glimpsed what love could be like, but her ex-boyfriend was right that she had never been able to trust him enough to open her heart to love him. It was not an excuse for cheating on her! Far from it. But, the more she thought about it, the more she realised that perhaps she had chosen someone who she knew she would walk away from, in one way or another, before he got too serious.

Why not? When her self-esteem as a woman was so low.

Well, these past few days had opened her eyes about a lot of things.

Ethan had made her realise that she had to find

her own way forward. Or face a lifetime of running away. Or, worse, running backwards.

A pair of herring gulls soared up from the edge of the chalk cliff on the wind, calling and squawking as they climbed higher and higher into the sky in front of Mari as she paused to watch them. They seemed to be mocking her and her weakness and lack of self-confidence.

Well, they were right about that, but she had made a start and there was a long way to go.

Head back, she closed her eyes and felt the wind blasting against the left side of her body, bringing with it the salty tang of sea and seaweed and all that she had grown up with and never once forgotten. She had walked this path at least once a day for the first sixteen years of her life and very little had changed.

Everything about this place and this moment was as different from her normal office life as anywhere in the world. But, as she stood there and listened to the sea and the bird calls and felt the wind and smelt the sea, she realised that in truth she had never left.

She had always carried this special place with her in her heart over these last ten years. It was the core of her sense of who she was and who she probably always would be. The self-confident girl who'd loved school and had a world of opportunity in front of her.

A smile crept onto Mari's face like a welcome friend. Strange. That idea had never even occurred to her until that moment. But it would explain why she felt so at peace here and why she felt compelled to go out on such a cold morning wearing the extra-long sheepskin coat that Ethan had given her when she could have stayed warm and snug in bed.

And of course there was one other reason why she had pulled on all of her winter clothing and borrowed Rosa's warm boots. She longed to see the house again so that she could start planning what improvements needed to be made.

Inhaling deeply, allowing the cold salty air to purge her lungs of the city smog, Mari finally opened her eyes and looked straight ahead of her.

She could just see the roof of the house, which

was set back a few hundred feet away from the cliff path and, with renewed vigour and purpose, she set off walking towards it, covering the short distance in fast long strides, her eyes fixed on the red tiles.

She turned her back on the sea, swung open the garden gate and stood and stared at her old home. And her breath froze in her lungs. Transfixed by shock and amazement at what she was looking at.

The pretty flower beds and neat lawn where she had once played and held tea parties was a brown, barren wasteland of waist-high weeds and wild bushes that choked the evergreen shrubs which had been chosen with such loving care to flourish in the harsh sea breezes. Broken pieces of furniture, glass and plastic bottles and rubbish of all kinds spewed out from an open dustbin, which was jammed against what was left of the broken wooden fence which had once been white and fresh and welcoming.

But it was the house itself which was the greatest shock. The front picture windows were gone—covered over by pieces of timber which stared out like grey eyes, cold and lifeless. The window frames and the front door were rotten and splintered, uncared for and useless and the guttering was waving loose in the wind from a broken wooden fascia.

Tiles were missing from the roof. There was a crack in the main chimney and a wild thistle was growing in the drainpipe.

Tears of grief and the biting wind pricked Mari's eyes and she heaved in a breath.

This was where she had wanted her lovely sister to make a home! This was the house she had longed to come back to! This was the house she had just bought with all of her savings, a loan from Ethan and a lot more than she could afford.

What had she been expecting? The same house she'd last seen when her mother was alive and they had walked along the cliff path on a hot summer day arm in arm and made light of the fact that the elderly couple who lived there were lovely people but gardening was not their strength? How could the house have deteriorated so fast? She had seen it only a few years ago and it had been nothing like this. But of course she had only seen it at a distance from the beach. Any closer was too painful.

Rosa had tried to warn her, but nothing could have prepared her for this amount of neglect. It was going to take months of work and more money than she had to make the house fit to live in.

Oh, Ethan. You were so right. Where was her secure and loving home? This certainly was not it.

Taking a couple of deep breaths, Mari pushed her way through the garden, being careful where she placed her feet, until she came to the kitchen door.

Once glance confirmed it. The door still had the original lock.

She glanced from side to side and immediately felt foolish because she had not seen anyone for the last ten minutes and she was the new owner on paper, then reached into her trouser pocket and pulled out a long brass key with an engraved handle.

Her father had made the keys and the lock by hand and given each of his family their own key. She had used this key once before, when she had sneaked in here with Ethan on the night of her sixteenth birthday, and she had kept it safe all of these years, waiting, just waiting, for this moment to use it again. *Time to see if it still fitted.*

Cautiously, she stretched out her hand, and then pulled it back again.

This was not her property yet! She couldn't simply go inside without asking permission. Could she?

The wind howled around her ankles and blew old leaves up in the air. She had come a long way to stand on this very special piece of earth. It was now or never.

Head up, Mari slowly and gently turned the key in the lock and felt the mechanism engage. The door itself had swollen in the winter rain and it took a little persuasion to open but, a few moments later, Mari Chance stepped inside the lobby and closed the door behind her.

She was back inside her home again.

This was the moment that had sustained her in the endless airport lounges and interminable meetings in boardrooms without windows. This should have been her great achievement.

She had come home. She was back.

And she felt sick at what she was looking at.

Her home was a shell of a building, dark, dank and gloomy and, in a moment of horror and barely suppressed claustrophobia, Mari stepped across the broken and filthy floor tiles they used to polish every Sunday evening to the window above the sink, and tugged hard at the plastic sheeting and cardboard which covered the window.

The flimsy sheets came away easily in her hands and pale February sunshine flooded into the dark kitchen, creating a spotlight around where she stood in the otherwise dark place. This window was north-facing and her mother had created stained glass panels in the top half of the window to add colour to the otherwise dull, flat light.

Mari blinked hard as the light flooded into the room through the large window that dominated the wall above the old ceramic sink.

Elsewhere in the stripped-out shell of a kitchen, there were dim shadows and corners of dark purple and grey above exposed electric wires and gas pipes, but Mari's attention was totally focused on the stained glass which, amazingly, wondrously, had survived intact and as bright and colourful as ever.

As she stepped closer, mesmerised, it was obvious that the glass in the window was not made from one continuous sheet of glass, but composed of separate smaller panels of varying thicknesses and slight colour differences which her mother had collected from old glass windows and painted by hand.

It was a garden with flowers and leaves of every colour in the spectrum.

Each piece was unique to itself but an essential component of the piece as they fitted together seamlessly to create the whole. Light hitting the thicker bevelled edges was deflected through multiple prisms to create rainbow spectra of colour which danced on the tiled floor at Mari's feet in a chaos of reds and pinks, pale violets and blues through to greens.

It was as though the light itself had taken on the colour of the glass, creating layers of different luminosity as it was diffracted and refracted and deflected through the uneven panels to produce a barrier between this space and the world outside.

Each panel was unique, creating a different illusion of the world beyond the glass.

On the other side of the glass, bare skeletons of trees bent towards the town in the howling wind from the sea, above the browns and russets of autumn colours. But here and there she could just make out the first signs of yellow daffodils and white snowdrops. Spring was on the way and in a few short weeks there would be new life and energy on the other side of the glass.

Mari sucked in a breath of cold, damp and dusty

air, coughed and exhaled slowly as she glanced around this empty, echoing and frigid room.

Her life was in that window.

The past was captured in her reflection on the glass for a few fleeting seconds until she moved away and the moment was lost. On *this* side of the glass was the present, and a girl whose reflection was looking back at her. And on the other side of the glass? That was where the future lay. Still hazy but with the promise of sunny days ahead.

But not here. Not in this room and not in this building. There was nothing for her here any more.

Mari closed her eyes and let the tears finally fall down her cheeks unchecked as she mourned the loss of everything she'd thought that she wanted.

What a fool she had been.

She pushed the heel of her hand tight against her forehead.

This was not the home she remembered and it never could be. Her mother was gone, and Rosa was moving away to create a new life for herself.

Almost blinded by tears and with a burning

throat, Mari forced herself to look around the bare walls and in an instant saw it for what it truly was. A shell of a house which had been cared for at one time when a family lived here, but that time was long gone.

Selfish, stupid girl. She had told herself that she wanted this house for Rosa, but that had been a pathetic delusion. This was all about what *she* wanted—for herself. Rosa was simply an excuse for justifying the years of hard work and sacrifice she had spent building up the finances to buy back this…what? This shell of a house filled with the echoes of ghosts and sadness? A tired and wrecked version of the home she had once known?

Mari leant back against the dirty painted kitchen wall, suddenly exhausted and bereft of ideas and energy.

She had to face the truth. It had never been the house she wanted. It had always been about the feeling of security and love. That was what she had hoped to bring back into her life through buying this building. As if a physical place could give her back her shattered self-confidence and make her open her heart to being loved.

Mari choked on the cold, dirty air she gulped into her lungs.

But there it was.

Ethan was right. She should be outside the window, looking at the new spring flowers, instead of inside her past, looking out in fear. But the idea was so hard to take.

Somehow she had to build up the strength to walk out of this room and this house, find Ethan and thank him again for loaning her the money and tell him it would not be needed after all.

It would be tough, embarrassing and humiliating, but that was what she had to do before she could move forward.

She had to accept the fact that she was not going to live here. The family who had wanted this house could buy it. And love it. And be happy here. This house needed a real family to transform it back into a loving home again, not a lonely single girl with delusions of bringing back the past.

Mari sniffled away the tears of grief at what she had lost and sacrificed, and she slid off her warm glove to dive into the pocket of Ethan's coat. Hopeful that he kept tissues somewhere down inside those extra-deep pockets.

Only instead of paper tissues her fingers closed around a package.

She pulled out a long oblong which had been gift-wrapped in bright red foil. A white adhesive label with Christmas holly leaves around the edges said: *A bit late for a Christmas present but I hope you like it. Thinking of you, Ethan.*

Mari swallowed down a lump in her throat the size of Dorset as she pressed her fingertip against the blue ink. She would have recognised his spidery-thin writing anywhere. Ethan had given her a present and not told her. Simply left it in his pocket for her to find.

She almost pushed it back into the pocket. She would be seeing him soon enough—he could present it to her properly then.

And yet... Her fingers smoothed the paper for

a second before ripping open the tape to find a slim black photo album.

Should she open it? Now? Here? In this cold, echoing place, so remote from the cosy, sunny bedroom with the stunning sea view in the house Ethan had built with such love for his parents?

Maybe there was something in here which would take her back there to that calm and intimate space where she had almost felt relaxed and open enough to reveal her feelings, in spirit if not in body?

Mari slowly unzipped the case and looked at the first photograph.

It was a bright colour print of the teenage Ethan she remembered from his first summer in Swanhaven, his arm wrapped around the junior sailing regatta trophy while his parents stood on either side of him, their arms draped around his shoulders. His pretty English mother in a printed summer dress, and his American father, tall and stately in shorts and T-shirt which never had seemed right on him.

All three of them were so happy. Their laughter captured forever in that fraction of a second.

This was his family. This was what he wanted to create for himself.

But it was the second photograph which undid her. It was a perfect shot of Kit and Ethan messing about on Ethan's boat with her dad at the helm. And there she was, laughing and happy. Standing on the jetty watching the two boys and her dad having fun. The kind of event that was such a commonplace part of her life over those last few summer holidays that she had taken it for granted and not once even thought of capturing it with her camera. And now she was so grateful that someone had. Probably Ethan's mum.

The tears streamed down her face unchecked. There was no point trying to stop them; it was much too late for that. Because the next photograph, and the one after that, was of Mari and Kit standing next to Ethan with their arms wrapped around one another's shoulders at the Swanhaven sailing school prize-giving, just smiling at the camera with their whole bright future ahead of them. So happy and content and living in the moment, with not a care in the world.

Oh, Ethan. Thank you for giving me this photograph.

Mari dropped her head down and slowly pulled the paper cover back over the photograph, blinking away her tears as best she could. The other photographs were for later. When she was secure in her own room with the door locked. On her own. Where she could weep in private.

Mari looked around the room. And then looked again—only harder and through eyes that seemed to be seeing it for what it truly was, and not through rose-tinted glasses which only showed what it had been like so long ago.

She had never felt lonelier in her life.

What was she doing here? In this cold house that echoed with the footsteps of ghosts instead of real living people?

There was only one place she needed to be at that moment, and it wasn't here with the ghosts.

She couldn't build a secure future for herself here. It was time to reconnect with that earlier version of herself that she had just been looking at. The version that Ethan remembered and the version that somehow, amazingly, he still saw in her.

And that thought dazzled her.

Ethan had offered her a chance to build a home with him. *A real home.* The kind of home she'd dreamt of creating. And she had been too woolly headed to see the genuine love and affection in that offer.

Mari pressed the heel of her hand hard against her forehead a couple of times.

Idiot. She was the one who did not deserve him. And now she had probably lost him. Which made her the biggest fool in the universe.

All she had to do was run as fast as she could and tell him that she trusted him with her love and her heart and her future. That was all.

CHAPTER ELEVEN

MARI wiped her eyes and was just about to push away from the wall when the sound of a car engine echoed around the house.

Oh, no. Someone had come to the house. *Drat!* Mari hurriedly tucked the photo album down inside the coat pocket, wiped her eyes, anxious for a stranger not to see her tears, and strode over to the back door and opened it wide.

'Hey, darlin', I'm thinking of moving to California. Do you know if there's any work for retired sailors down there? Because you know what they say? All the nice girls love a sailor.'

Ethan Chandler stood outside on the stone step; he was smiling, but his body revealed the tension and anxiety he was trying to hide. His eyes flicked across her face, taking in the tears and trauma before he spoke again. 'Hi. Thought I might find you here.'

She couldn't speak.

He was here. Just when she needed him most. And he was here. *For her.*

So she did the most natural thing in the world. A gesture she had wanted to make a thousand times before.

She leant forward and gently, gently pressed her lips onto his in thanks, before wrapping her arms around his neck and hugging him for all she was worth, pressing her body hard against the muscles of his chest so that she could feel his heart against hers. Holding him so tight in the hope that all of his strength and courage and trust in her could seep across the few layers of clothing that separated them and she could finally tell him how much he had come to mean to her.

Words were impossible, and his own response came in a husky whisper.

'Sorry I missed you at the house. I was too busy trying to come up with some cunning plan to entice you back to Florida with me. My parents have agreed to help me set up a trust fund for a sailing school where we can take the teenagers on longer sea voyages lasting a few months each summer. There will be experts on board to help with their problems. And I can show them what sailing really means.' He paused for a second, and then lowered his hands to cup her face before he went on. 'I want to call it the Kit Chance Sailing Trust. If that's okay with you.'

She looked into his eyes in shock. 'You want to teach sailing in memory of Kit? Oh, Ethan. Of course it's okay.'

Her eyes pricked with the sharp acid of fresh tears as his fingers wiped them away. He scanned her face. 'And now you've gone quiet on me again. What are you thinking?'

The words tumbled out on a breath. 'I was standing here feeling sorry for myself. Alone. And pathetic. And at the same time you were working on the best possible way I can think of for Kit to be remembered. Oh, Ethan, I have been such a fool. Thank you. Thank you for letting me go through with the biggest mistake of my life.'

She lifted her head and glanced around. 'I don't need this house to give me a false sense of security any longer. I've decided to take the initiative and accept redundancy from my company so I can make a fresh start. I'm not afraid of being rejected any longer. I can find work and trust myself to see it through. And I know I must sound totally crazy right now, but that's what I am going to do.'

Ethan eased back and took both of her hands in his, the gentleness and tenderness of his touch filling her heart with hope that he did not think her a complete idiot.

'No, it's not crazy. It's the most amazing thing I've ever heard in my life!'

Ethan pretended to glance around the room; only his thumbs were still stroking the back of her hands and, as he turned back to face her, he lifted her hands to his lips and kissed the knuckles. Kissed them as though they were the most precious things in the world to him, his eyes fixed on hers.

'Are you sure, Mari? Are you sure about giving up this house?'

All she could manage was a nod. 'You've shown me that it is possible to move on and make your own happiness. And that's what I want to do. Create my own future from what I want and need. And it's not this house. Another family can make it their home.'

Their eyes locked. She was hypnotised. Unable to break away.

'You're an amazing woman, Mari. I never thought you could surprise me any more, but you have done. Any man would want to have you in his life. Want you in his bed. Make you the last thing he sees at night. The woman he wakes up with every morning.'

She knew he was smiling by the creases in the corners of both eyes.

'I was a boy who thought that he would never be good enough for someone as beautiful and clever as you. Will you give me a chance to prove that I have become a better man who is finally worthy of you? Because you were right. I have been running from my emotions for far too long. It's time I faced up to my feelings and told you that the only thing I need is you.'

Mari closed her eyes as his hands moved back to her waist and opened them just as he pressed his forehead onto hers. 'It broke my heart when you left, Ethan, and I blamed you for everything that had happened, but it wasn't ever about you. It was about me and how guilty I felt about wanting you to care about me. I was so angry and lonely. Rosa and our mother were relying on me to take care of things when our lives fell apart. I had lost my brother and then my father, and then you were gone. I had to protect myself from being rejected all over again. Do you see? I had to keep my feelings inside, just to get through each and every day.'

'Then let me show you that I'm back in your life and I am here to stay for as long as you want me to. I'm not just any man. I'm the man who wants to hold you in his arms and have you by my side every day. I want to spend the rest of my life showing you how much I need you. How much you mean to me. And how very, very beautiful you are. Can you trust me, Mari? Can you open your heart and let me love you?'

He swept both hands down from her forehead, smoothing her hair down, over and over, building the strength to say the words, his eyes focused on hers, his voice broken and ragged with such intensity that it was impossible for her to reply. For once she had to listen.

'I love you, Marigold Chance. I've loved you since I was twelve years old. I walked into your mother's kitchen—this kitchen we're standing in now, a lonely boy in a new town who was trying so hard to find a place for himself in the world, and then you turned to me and smiled.'

Tears filled his eyes as he stroked her face.

'And I knew that everything was going to be okay. Because I had a friend who…'

His voice broke and he could only drop his hands to wrap around her back, pressing his body closer to hers, his head into her neck, where his breath came hot and fast from his heaving chest as he fought back fifteen years of suppressed desires and hopes.

She could feel the pressure of his lips on her skin, but everything was suddenly a blur. If only the fireworks would stop going off in her head, she might have a chance of making sense of those magical words. Except that rockets seemed to be exploding all around her in a glorious display of brilliant bursts of colour.

Ethan loved her. Ethan Chandler. Loved. Her.

With all of the strength she thought she had lost, Mari slid her hands from his waist up the front of his chest, resisting the temptation to rip his shirt off, and felt this man's heart thumping wildly under the cloth. His shirt was sweaty, and she could feel the moist hair on his chest under her fingers and, as she moved to his throat, the pulse rang out under her touch.

She forced her head back, away from his body, inches away from this remarkable, precious man who had exposed his deepest dreams to her.

'I've looked everywhere for the missing parts, but nobody was able to mend it,' she whispered.

'And how could they, when it was right here all of the time? You were simply holding them safe for me. And…and I knew you were. I was just so scared that you would break my heart all over again. So scared.'

Her hand came up to stroke Ethan's face as he looked at her in silence, his chest heaving as he forced air into his lungs. 'Will you come and live with me, Mari? I can build you a house anywhere you like, but only you can make it a home, Mari. Only you. You can work from home, an office, a boat, anywhere you like, as long as we are together.'

His voice was full of excitement and energy, the desire burning in every word.

His eyes flicked across her face, trying to gauge her reaction.

'Will you be my partner, my lover, and the mother of my children? Can you do that? Can you take a chance at happiness with me?'

She gasped in a breath as the tears streamed down her face, knowing that he was saying the only words she had waited a lifetime to hear.

'Yes.'

He looked back at her and his mouth dropped open in shock. 'Yes?'

'Yes.' She laughed. 'Yes, yes, yes. Oh, Ethan, I love you so much.'

She had barely got the words out of her mouth before she was silenced by the pressure of his mouth, which would have knocked her backwards if not for the strong arms that pressed her body to his. Eyes closed, she revelled in the glorious sensation of his lips, tongue and body. Lights were going on in parts of her body where she had not known switches existed. She felt as if she was floating on air.

Her eyes flicked open to find that she *was* floating on air, as Ethan hoisted her up by the waist, twirling her around and around, two grown-up people hooting with joy, oblivious to the freezing cold, dank and dusty air. A kaleidoscope of happiness, colour and light.

Then she slid back down his body, her extended arms caressed lovingly by strong hands. And she wanted to be alone with this man and show him how she felt about him.

Marigold Chance was going to miss her flight. And take the first step on the greatest adventure of her life.

Mari looked into Ethan's smiling face, stunned by the joy she had brought to this precious man, and grinned.

'Don't you just love families? Let's go home, Ethan. Wherever you are in the world—that is my home and I don't want to spend another day away from you. Take me home, Ethan. Take me home.'

EPILOGUE

MARI CHANDLER looked up from the screen of her laptop just as Ethan helped one of his teenagers down from the rigging on the *Swanhaven Princess* and her foolish heart leapt and skipped just at the sight of the man she loved so very much.

Ethan was laughing, head back with such reckless delight at what his young sailor had achieved.

His passion for sailing was so infectious that he seemed to be able to break down any barrier. This boy had been afraid of heights only a few weeks ago when they left Swanhaven and now look at him! Ethan did amazing and wonderful work. She was so proud of what they had achieved.

Mari stretched her arms out above her head and arched her back like a cat to release her shoulders before sighing in sweet contentment. Warmth oozed back at her from the sun-baked cushion and polished wood and she sat back, eyes half-closed, just happy to enjoy the sensation of the warm light wind on her face as the wooden training ship ripped through the calm waters of the Aegean Sea.

It was hard to believe that a few months ago she had never known what it felt like to dive among corals and exotic striped fish she had only ever seen before in an aquarium. Now she spent her afternoons snorkelling with the teenagers and helping them learn to swim in the crystal-clear, warm shallow waters, safe in the knowledge that by her side was the only guide she could ever want. Ethan. *Her Ethan.*

There was a cheer from the cluster of teenagers around the helm and she opened her eyes and smiled for a second before reaching for her camera so she could capture this moment—for the boy who had just climbed to the top rigging, for his family and also for the online weblog which was already starting to create a huge internet following. The Kit Chance Sailing Trust was more than just an idea—it had become an international reality. This was her life and her job now.

And it was all down to the vision and passion of the man she was looking at now. The man who had half turned away from the group so that he could look at her. Simply look at her. And the love in those blue eyes the colour of the Greek sky was almost too much for her to take in.

Every day, just when she thought that she could not be more proud of Ethan or could love him more, he proved her wrong. He gave her so much. His love, his warmth and his total belief in her ability and talents. Sometimes it seemed like a happy dream, interrupted by the occasional teenage fight, or tantrums where the teenagers needed their mother on the other end of an internet telephone. The usual sort of thing which went on in any extended family.

And she adored it all.

The sun was starting to go down over the horizon in a blaze of incredible colour creating a miraculous sunset of orange flame, with shades of deep apricots over dark duck-egg-blues and greens. It felt as though the sky itself was celebrating the end of a perfect hot, sunny day in the Aegean.

But it was nothing compared to the warmth in Ethan's smile as he strolled over to the wooden table and sat down next to her, his arm around her bare shoulder. The feeling of his lips pressed against the side of her neck thrilled her with a delicious shiver of love and excitement, and the connection deep inside her tightened like a piece of taut rigging line, pulling her even closer to the man she had given her heart to.

'Do we really have to leave? I wish this could go on for ever,' she whispered and gently swept a loose curl of bleached blond hair back over one ear from his tanned forehead.

'It could—' he grinned and tilted his head '—but my dad has already booked himself onto the next sailing course around the Caribbean we promised them at the wedding. He can't wait for us to sail the *Princess* back to Swanhaven ready for the trip back to Florida. I can see a lot of sailing lessons on the horizon crossing the Atlantic. We have a lot of father-and-son time to catch up on.'

'It was a stroke of genius suggesting to your parents that they should take over the running of the sailing charity. Your mother is the most amazing fund-raiser and they both love working with the teenagers,' Mari replied with a chuckle. 'We're lucky to have them.'

'It was the best decision they ever made. Swanhaven or Florida. They love it. Speaking of which, have you heard from Rosa? We need T-shirts, sweaters, shorts—everything. The kids go through clothing faster than I ever thought possible.'

Mari tapped Ethan once on the end of his nose. 'Relax—she e-mailed me this morning while you were working on the sails. It's all in hand. Rosa adores her new job, the new sailing-wear line has taken off and I have a feeling that the wedding dress she made me is not going to be her last. Perhaps you were right? Perhaps we might have two lady entrepreneurs in the family.' Mari stroked Ethan's face and watched his eyes flutter half-closed in pleasure and languorous delight. 'And that family includes you now, Mr Chandler.'

'Does it really, Mrs Chandler? Well, that could be a problem because the only family I want is right here on the deck wearing a very fetching bikini and a cheeky grin.' He shot a glance back at the teenage boys who were sniggering, winking at him or giving them a thumbs up. 'Or do you think that is being too selfish, seeing as we have an audience?'

'Selfish?' Mari pretended to consider the question before crossing her arms around Ethan's neck and pulling him closer. 'No, my love. Wherever you are is my home and my true family. Even if that home is in the galley of a wooden training ship surrounded by two dozen teenagers for a couple of months at a time. Thank heavens for modern technology and satellite communication systems.'

'Thank heavens,' he repeated, his nose nuzzling her throat for a second before getting back to his feet and drawing her up by his side. 'I did promise the kids that they could choose the music for our last night in the Aegean. And guess what? It looks like we'll be sailing into harbour to the tune of the latest trance tracks. Do you think the Greek islands are ready for that?'

Ethan moved to pull away but Mari stayed right where she was. 'Ready? Perhaps not. But this is our family. And families stick together.'

And her loving husband took a firmer grasp of her hand and they turned to face the cheering teenagers, ready for anything that life could throw at them. *Together.*

* * * * *

Mills & Boon® Large Print
March 2012

THE POWER OF VASILII
Penny Jordan

THE REAL RIO D'AQUILA
Sandra Marton

A SHAMEFUL CONSEQUENCE
Carol Marinelli

A DANGEROUS INFATUATION
Chantelle Shaw

HOW A COWBOY STOLE HER HEART
Donna Alward

TALL, DARK, TEXAS RANGER
Patricia Thayer

THE BOY IS BACK IN TOWN
Nina Harrington

JUST AN ORDINARY GIRL?
Jackie Braun

0212 Rom LP